FROM THE
NANCY DREW FILES

THE CASE: A plan to convert the old Lakeside Inn into a chic club has been targeted for sabotage.

CONTACT: Ned's friend Andrew has sunk a small fortune into the job—and now the project threatens to sink him.

SUSPECTS: Andrew Lockwood—*Does he plan to cut his losses . . . and cut a deal with the insurance company?*

Julie Ross—*Has resentment led Andrew's ex-fiancée to seek a measure of revenge?*

Master Blaster—*is the devious deejay spinning a plot to insure that the club never opens?*

COMPLICATIONS: Not only does Nancy have to deal with the investigation, she has to deal with Ned's anger: He can't believe she could even suspect Andrew of wrongdoing.

Books in The Nancy Drew Files® Series

Available from ARCHWAY Paperbacks

THE
NANCY DREW
FILES™

Case 67

NOBODY'S
BUSINESS

CAROLYN KEENE

AN ARCHWAY PAPERBACK
Published by POCKET BOOKS
New York   London   Toronto   Sydney   Tokyo   Singapore

AN ARCHWAY PAPERBACK *Original*

An Archway Paperback published by
POCKET BOOKS, a division of Simon & Schuster Inc.
1230 Avenue of the Americas, New York, NY 10020

ISBN: 0-671-73071-1

First Archway Paperback printing January 1992

10 9 8 7 6 5 4 3 2 1

NANCY DREW, AN ARCHWAY PAPERBACK and colophon
are registered trademarks of Simon & Schuster Inc.

THE NANCY DREW FILES is a trademark
of Simon & Schuster Inc.

Cover art by Tom Galasinski

Printed in the U.S.A.

IL 6+

NOBODY'S BUSINESS

Chapter

One

WOULD YOU take a look at this place?" Bess Marvin exclaimed. "It's so romantic!"

Nancy Drew steered her blue Mustang into the parking lot of the Lakeside Inn and parked. "You think everything's romantic," she teased, turning to grin at her best friend. "Inns, movies, can openers, rutabagas . . ."

Giggling, Bess zipped up her fuchsia jacket and pulled her matching hat down over her long blond hair. "In this case you have to admit I'm right," she insisted, getting out of the car.

Nancy climbed out of the driver's side and stretched her long legs, which were stiff from the hour-long drive from the girls' hometown of

1

River Heights, in the Midwest. The cold January wind whipped through Nancy's reddish blond hair and numbed her cheeks and hands.

"The inn *is* beautiful," she agreed, her blue eyes gazing at the rambling old stone building nestled in a dense thicket of trees at the edge of a lake.

Two stories tall, the Lakeside Inn had turrets and gables and chimneys poking up from the sloping red clay roof, and stone terraces outside each window. To the right of the inn Nancy spotted a gazebo, a boathouse, and a pier that extended into the frozen silver lake.

"I can't wait to see the inside," Bess said. "Ned told you Andrew has already totally gutted it, right?"

Just hearing the name of her longtime boyfriend, Ned Nickerson, made Nancy want to see him. She'd seen him only once since he'd been home on winter break from Emerson College. Ned had been spending most of his time helping to renovate the Lakeside Inn. Andrew Lockwood, a friend of Ned's who had recently graduated from Emerson, was doing the renovation for his father, who owned the inn.

"I'm glad you suggested we pitch in and help with the renovation," Nancy told Bess, pulling up the hood of her kelly green parka. "This way Andrew gets two extra pairs of hands, I get to spend three whole weeks with Ned . . ."

"And I get to meet Andrew," Bess finished.

"George is going to be sorry she missed out." George Fayne, Bess's cousin and Nancy's friend, was on a ski trip in Colorado with her parents.

Laughing, Nancy locked the car, and the two girls walked across the lot toward the inn. There were only a few cars besides Nancy's, as well as a beat-up red school bus with "TeenWorks" painted along the side. Up ahead a semicircular driveway led to the inn's front entrance, which consisted of broad granite steps and a pair of fifteen-foot-high wooden doors.

"There you are!" a deep, familiar male voice called a moment later. "What took you so long?"

Despite the cold, Nancy felt warm all over as she looked up to see her tall boyfriend, wearing jeans and a flannel shirt, standing in the inn's doorway. With his brown eyes and wavy brown hair, he looked more handsome than ever. Nancy broke into a run, her long legs speeding her up the curved driveway and into Ned's outstretched arms.

"I missed you," she whispered into his ear as he held her close. Then she tilted back her head, and their lips met in a lingering kiss.

"That was definitely a greeting worth waiting for," Ned said, his brown eyes sparkling down at her. "Hi, Bess," he added, giving her a kiss on the cheek. "Come on in and meet Andrew, you guys. He's been dying to meet my girlfriend, the world-famous detective."

Nancy blushed slightly. She had solved dozens

3

of cases, but she was still embarrassed by the attention she sometimes received. "For the next few days don't think of me as a detective," she said quickly. "Think of me as a pair of helping hands. You're not the only one on break, Ned."

"Sorry we're late," Bess added. "I had to run some errands for my mother."

Nancy and Bess followed Ned into the large high-ceilinged lobby. The floor was covered with sawdust, but Nancy could still see how elegant the decor had once been. On either side of the lobby an elegant staircase with a mahogany banister curved gracefully up to the second floor. An open doorway framed by marble columns led to a long hallway that ran from left to right.

Ned showed Nancy and Bess a metal rack in the lobby where they could leave their jackets. "I'll give you a complete tour later," he told them. "Basically all the rooms facing the front are offices, and the rooms facing the lake are for guests. There's going to be a kitchen, a dining room, a ballroom, and a library, too."

"Sounds pretty grand," Nancy said, feeling her nose start to itch from all the sawdust. She searched in her jeans pocket for a tissue and found one just before she had to sneeze.

Bess nodded toward the curved stairways and asked, "What's upstairs?"

"Twenty bedrooms, each with a private bathroom," Ned told her.

"Sounds like a lot of work," Nancy commented.

Ned let out a long breath. "Tell me about it. The framework for the walls is already up, though, and we're almost finished with the electrical work," he explained. "We've just started the plumbing. Then we plasterboard the walls."

With a worried look at Ned, Bess said, "I hope you don't expect me to know exactly what I'm doing."

"Andrew's got a great foreman," Ned told her. "He'll tell you exactly what to do. Come on, let's go meet him. Andrew and some of the others are in the ballroom."

He led them through the marble columns and made a left down the hall, which was lit only by work lights hanging from overhead beams. The corridor ran the length of the inn. Its walls were made of stone, Nancy saw, with wooden framework built against them. Electrical cables were laced through the framework.

"Wow, this place is huge," Bess said, pausing as they went through a wide doorway. Nancy stopped next to her and looked around.

The ballroom was fifty feet long and had a vaulted ceiling that stretched the full height of the inn's two stories. An old chandelier still hung from the ceiling, but it didn't seem to be working. The room was lit by freestanding work lights. A large overhanging balcony jutted out of the left wall, about fifteen feet up. The ballroom floor was covered with large drop cloths, but a folded corner revealed a marble floor underneath. Loud, funky music blasted from somewhere overhead.

Half a dozen teenagers on ladders were scattered around the room, attaching electrical cable to wooden frameworks like the ones Nancy had seen in the hall. A few other teens sawed copper pipes over wooden sawhorses. Several more people stood in the middle of the room, talking and looking at an unscrolled blueprint set up on a table made of two wooden sawhorses and a few sheets of plywood.

"Andrew!" Ned called over the music. "Nancy and Bess are here."

A tall young man stepped away from the group around the blueprint and walked toward Nancy, Ned, and Bess. His straight black hair hung over his high forehead, and his hazel eyes were magnified by a pair of round, wire-rimmed glasses. He wore jeans and a black sweatshirt with white lettering that read Melborne Community Theater.

"Andrew Lockwood, meet my girlfriend, Nancy Drew," Ned said, putting his arm around Nancy. "And this is her friend Bess Marvin."

Andrew gave the girls a warm smile. "It's really nice of you to pitch in with the renovation," he told them. "At the rate we're going, I can use all the help I can get." He sighed, and several worry lines appeared on his forehead.

"What do you mean?" Nancy asked. "Aren't things going well?"

Andrew looked over his shoulder, as if to make sure no one else was near enough to overhear. "These renovations are taking a lot longer than I expected," he confided, frowning. "They're costing a lot more, too."

"I'm sorry to hear that," Nancy told him.

"I wish we'd come earlier," Bess added. "I think working here will be a lot of fun. This inn is definitely going to be great."

From the dazzling smile Bess gave Andrew, Nancy could tell that getting to know Andrew was what Bess was really looking forward to.

Andrew didn't seem to notice her interest, however. He merely shrugged and said, "I hope so. My father will kill me if I don't come through on this within the budget he gave me."

His last words were drowned out as the music switched to a new song with a catchy rhythm.

"Great music," Nancy told Andrew. She nodded toward a teenage girl with waist-length blond hair who moved to the beat as she worked on her ladder. "I see it helps keep your workers going."

"They're so young," Bess added. "They look like they're our age."

Andrew nodded. "They are," he said. "My dad gave me a very limited budget for the renovation, so to save money, I'm using TeenWorks. It's a vocational program for local teens, run by the county. The kids learn skills like plumbing, electrical work, carpentry . . . and they earn money at the same time. Though, of course, they don't earn as much as union workers."

"Don't they go to school?" Bess asked.

"This *is* school, some of the time," Andrew said. "They have classroom training, too, but a lot of their education is on the job."

"And that's where they *really* learn, of course," said a voice from behind Nancy's shoulder.

Turning, Nancy saw an attractive woman who looked to be in her early thirties and had shoulder-length red hair and a light dusting of freckles on her nose. She wore a green silk blouse that brought out the green of her eyes, faded blue jeans that showed her slim figure, and shiny black lizard-skin cowboy boots.

"Nancy, Bess, this is Colleen Morgan," Andrew said. "She's the coordinator for TeenWorks."

Colleen laughed. "What Andrew really means is that I'm a bored housewife looking for a way to kill time," she said, "so I volunteer."

Raising his eyebrows skeptically, Andrew said, "'Bored housewife' is hardly the term I'd use. Colleen is selflessly devoting her time to this project even though she could be jetting around the world," he explained to Nancy and Bess. "You see, she's married to Frederick Morgan— of Morgan Lumber, Morgan Steel, Morgan Financial Services—"

"Enough!" Colleen shushed Andrew, waving a

well-manicured hand that was heavy with rings. "You're giving away my dirty secret. Well, right now I need to be jetting around this building. I want to see how the rest of the gang is doing upstairs." With another wave of her hand, she headed for the archway leading out of the ballroom.

Nancy was impressed that this wealthy woman cared about helping others. She couldn't help thinking it would have made more sense if Colleen wore a sweatshirt and sneakers rather than her expensive outfit. Then again, maybe they *were* her casual clothes.

"Yo, Andrew," a wiry teenage boy spoke up as he entered the ballroom and sauntered toward them. He had razor-cut platinum blond hair and wore a baggy, untucked shirt, black jeans, and a pair of purple hightop sneakers.

"I hate to bother you," the boy said, "but it's sort of important."

"Sure, Blaster," Andrew said. "I want you to meet my friends, anyway."

"Blaster?" Bess asked, looking perplexed. "Is that really your name?"

The boy flashed Bess a cocky grin and said, "It's Master Blaster, the music meister."

"Blaster's our deejay," Andrew explained. "He keeps music playing on his tape player while we're working."

"The hottest mix in town," Master Blaster added, winking at Bess. "I'm wired for sound—

when I'm not doing the electrical wiring for the inn."

Bess's cheeks turned pink, and Nancy had to smile. It looked as if Bess had actually met a guy who was even more of a flirt than she was!

"Blaster's the assistant to the master electrician," Andrew informed them. "He graduated from TeenWorks in June, and now he's on staff." Turning back to Blaster, he said, "So what's up? Don't tell me there's another problem."

Blaster looked apologetic. "You told me to come to you if any more tools were missing. Well, now I can't find my soldering iron, and Natalia Diaz told me she's missing her three-eighths drill bit *and* the drill."

Andrew's lips pressed together in a thin line. "I can't believe this," he muttered. "Every day it's something else. Tools keep disappearing, some of the wiring got cut in the dining room, and someone tore up some of the floorboards upstairs."

Nancy didn't know much about construction, but something about these accidents seemed weird. "Where was your soldering iron the last time you saw it?" she asked Master Blaster.

"Upstairs, in one of the bedrooms," he replied. "My boss, Eddie, called me into another room for about two minutes. When I got back, the iron was gone."

"And you didn't see or hear anybody?" Nancy asked.

Blaster shook his head. "I don't know what it is," he said. "I've worked on a lot of jobs before, but I've never seen one where so many things went wrong." He fixed his dark brown eyes on Andrew. "Maybe somebody doesn't like you, man."

Suddenly a mischievous twinkle lit up Blaster's eyes, and he added, "Or maybe it's the Lakeside ghost."

"Ghost?" Bess echoed. She looked as if she didn't know whether to be amused or scared.

Blaster nodded. "Sure. An old place like this is definitely haunted," he said, doing a dance step in time to the beat of the music blasting overhead.

"Don't listen to him," Andrew told Bess, rolling his eyes. "He's just babbling."

"Sorry," Blaster said. "Oops! I think I hear Eddie calling me." With that he bounded out of the room.

Turning to Andrew, Nancy inquired, "So, what about this ghost story?"

"It's not really much of a story," Andrew said, shrugging. "The inn was built over a hundred years ago as a popular society resort. Lots of big business moguls from Chicago would come here and stay all summer."

"I can see why," Bess said, letting her blue eyes gaze around the room. "You can tell how elegant it must have been."

"I hope it will be again, too," Andrew said.

"Anyway, two of the families that came here, the Aarons and the Murrays, were bitter rivals because they owned competing oil companies. The families never even spoke to each other until one summer when Lawrence Aaron fell in love with Rosalie Murray."

"Uh-oh," Nancy said. "I can see where this is going."

Andrew grinned at her. "You guessed it. They wanted to get married," he said. "Their parents threatened to disown them, but they went ahead with the plans, anyway. The wedding was scheduled to take place in this very room."

"What happened?" Bess asked.

"The night before the wedding, there was a big fire at the inn," Andrew went on, "and Rosalie disappeared. The inn was nearly destroyed."

"What about Rosalie?" Ned asked. "Did they ever find her?"

"No," Andrew told him. "Some say she died in the fire, brokenhearted, and that her ghost still haunts the inn. But, of course, that's totally ridiculous. Everybody knows there's no such thing as—"

He broke off as the amplified music stopped in the middle of a song. A moment later a chilling, anguished wail echoed in the ballroom.

"Aaaaaaagh!"

The sound made Nancy's skin crawl and sent icy shivers running down her back.

"Aaaaaaagh!" The wailing continued, even

louder now, and Nancy jumped as it was echoed by a frightened scream from Bess. Up on their ladders and down on the floor, the teenage workers looked around anxiously.

"Oh, no!" Bess shrieked. "The ghost is right here in this room!"

Chapter

Two

"LET'S GET OUT of here!" Bess shouted over the eerie shrieking. Her cry was echoed by some of the teen workers.

With a hand on Bess's arm Nancy looked quickly around the ballroom. "Calm down," she told everyone. "I'm sure there's an explanation."

"Maybe this place really *is* haunted," the blond girl on the ladder suggested.

The wails stopped as abruptly as they'd started, leaving a ringing echo in the huge room.

"It's haunted all right," Andrew said grimly. "By a practical joker with a bad sense of humor."

Nancy had been thinking exactly the same thing. Pointing up to the balcony, she said, "The music seemed to be coming from there, and it

14

stopped right before the wailing started. My guess is that someone's been playing with your stereo, Andrew. Can we go up there and check it out?"

"Good idea," Andrew said, heading for a door set in the wall beneath the balcony.

He led Nancy, Ned, and Bess through the door and up a dimly lit staircase. It smelled damp and musty, and cobwebs dangled from the ceiling. The group's footsteps echoed noisily as they climbed.

When they reached the top, Andrew led them through an open doorway and onto the balcony. A compact stereo system sat on the floor, its components stacked on top of each other and connected by wires to two large speakers.

Kneeling down in front of the stereo, Nancy placed a hand on top of the tape deck. It was still warm, even though it was turned off. Only one of the two cassette decks had a tape in it. Nancy pushed the Eject button and found a cassette hand-labeled Master Blaster's Super Mix. When she popped it back into the cassette deck and pressed the Play button, the same dance music that had been playing when they'd come in blasted from the speakers.

"Did you find anything, Nan?" Bess asked.

Nancy tapped the empty second cassette player. "It's what I didn't find that's got me wondering," she said. "Someone could have sneaked up these stairs and put in another tape of the wailing

15

sounds we heard. Then the person could have taken the tape out and sneaked out again."

"Blaster isn't going to be too happy that someone changed his program," Andrew commented, frowning. "In fact, I'm surprised he hasn't come up here, yelling like a maniac. He hates it when anyone else touches his sound system."

Nancy stared at Andrew. "I wonder why he didn't show up," she mused. Unless he was the one responsible, she added to herself. Blaster had left the ballroom a few minutes before the ghostly wails replaced the music. That was long enough for him to have changed the tapes himself.

Then she shook herself. Stop playing detective, she told herself. You're on vacation, remember?

Nancy looked up as Andrew let out a groan. "Every time there's a delay like this, it costs me money," he said, taking off his glasses and wearily rubbing his eyes. "My father's going to kill me if I go over budget."

"Don't worry about him," Ned said, clapping Andrew on the back.

As Ned spoke consolingly to Andrew, Nancy wandered toward the shadowy stairway. Just before the entrance to the balcony, she noticed an alcove she hadn't seen before. A metal plate was attached to the wall there, with several black dials on it and some holes with bare wires sticking out. It looked like a master light switch.

Before she could take a closer look, Nancy heard a sound on the stairs below her. She froze

16

and listened. Were those retreating footsteps? Maybe the intruder was still nearby.

"Where are you going?" Bess asked as Nancy ran from the balcony.

"I'll be right back," Nancy called over her shoulder. She rushed down the stairs two at a time, trying to make out a figure in the darkness.

When Nancy got to the bottom, she realized that there was a hallway that led from the ballroom. The footsteps sounded far away, but Nancy ran blindly down the hallway toward them. Suddenly she saw a rectangle of daylight appear in the distance and a silhouetted figure pass through it before the hall went dark again. It was a door leading outside.

Picking up her pace, Nancy barreled the rest of the way down the hall, flung open the door, and felt a cold rush of winter air slap her in the face. She was standing a few yards from the rocky shore of Moon Lake.

Hearing a snapping, crackling sound to her right, Nancy turned and saw a slender girl with dark curly hair running toward a grove of trees. Though the girl was far away, Nancy could also see that she had a single streak of coppery red in the middle of her curls.

Nancy took off after the girl, but she kept losing sight of her among the dense evergreen trees. Then the girl disappeared altogether. Nancy stopped to listen, but the woods were still except for the sound of her own heavy breathing.

With a sigh of frustration, she trudged back to the inn. The sun was already setting over the lake, bathing the stone building in an orange glow.

The back door was ajar. As Nancy approached it from the rear, she pulled it open—then stopped short. "Blaster, what are you doing here?" she asked in surprise.

The wiry teenager looked just as surprised to see her. "Just, uh, getting some air," he mumbled. Then, turning his back to Nancy, he headed down the dark hallway toward the ballroom.

It was clear Blaster was covering something up. Could he have had something to do with the eerie music, or with the girl who'd just run off?

Nancy hurried to catch up with him. "Did you see anyone just now?" she asked. "A girl with curly dark hair?"

"I didn't see anybody," Blaster said, striding the last few steps to the door and throwing it open. "Like I said, I was just getting some air." Hands in his pockets, he walked past the other teenagers and left the ballroom.

"What happened to you, Nancy?" Bess asked as she, Ned, and Andrew hurried over to her. "You're sweating!"

Quickly Nancy described what she'd seen, adding Blaster's strange behavior. "Does that girl sound like anyone working here?" Nancy asked Andrew.

Andrew glanced uneasily at Nancy. "Not that I know of," he replied after a moment.

"Wait a minute," Ned said, turning to Andrew. "That sounds exactly like Jul—"

Andrew cut off Ned with an angry glare.

"Sorry," Ned said, backing off. "I know you don't like to talk about her."

"Talk about who?" Nancy asked. "If you have any idea who she might be, you should tell us. She could be the one causing the problems here."

Ignoring Nancy, Andrew said gruffly, "It's five o'clock—quitting time. Why don't you guys go home and meet me back here tomorrow morning at eight?"

Nancy studied Andrew's tensely set jaw and the troubled look in his hazel eyes. What had come over him all of a sudden?

"You know, Andrew," Bess said, laying a hand on his arm, "I feel so embarrassed at the way I freaked out over the ghost. I hope you won't hold it against me."

Andrew looked right over the top of Bess's head at two teenage boys pretending to duel with strips of wood, banging them together with loud clacks. "Hey!" Andrew shouted, striding away from Nancy and her friends. "Stop messing around!"

"Oh, well," Bess whispered to Nancy. "I guess I didn't make much of an impression on Andrew."

"Don't let it get you down, Bess," Ned said. "You wouldn't have had a chance with him no matter what."

"Oh, great," Bess said, rolling her eyes. "That's comforting."

"No, that's not what I meant." He shot Andrew a quick look, then said, "Let's go get some dinner. I'll explain then. There's a great Mexican restaurant right up the road."

"Thanks for driving me, by the way," Ned said. "I can't believe my car's in the shop—again."

"No problem," Nancy said, slipping her arm around his waist. "The more time we spend together, the better I like it. Consider me your personal chauffeur for the next three weeks."

After waving goodbye to Andrew, the three of them got their jackets in the lobby, then went out to Nancy's Mustang. Ned directed Nancy to a narrow road that curved around the lake. In a few minutes they saw a cluster of small buildings, among them a crafts boutique called A Show of Hands, a post office, a bank, a small grocery store, and a Mexican restaurant, Paquito's.

Nancy parked, then she and her friends entered the tiny restaurant. A half dozen wooden booths filled the room, and the stone walls were draped with colorfully striped blankets.

"So tell me," Nancy said, sliding into a wooden booth beside Ned. "What's the story with Andrew? What's he hiding about this J person?"

"He's not hiding anything, exactly," Ned began. "It just hurts him to talk about it. A few weeks ago his fiancée, Julie Ross, broke up with him. He's been really devastated ever since. I don't think he could even look at another girl."

"And you think that girl I saw was Julie?" Nancy asked.

Ned nodded. "She fits the description perfectly. How many girls have brown hair with a red streak running through it? And she works right next door here, at A Show of Hands. It's just a short walk from the inn."

"Why did Julie break up with him?" Bess asked. "He seems like a nice guy."

Ned plucked a tortilla chip from a bowl on the table and dipped it in salsa. "She got tired of waiting for Andrew to make up his mind," he explained. "See, Mr. Lockwood doesn't just own the inn. He owns a lot of real estate around here, and he wants to bring Andrew into the business now that he's out of college."

"I get it," Nancy put in. "This renovation project is like a trial run."

"Exactly," Ned told her. "The thing is, Andrew really wanted to be an actor. He planned to marry Julie and move with her to Los Angeles. He was going to start auditioning and taking acting classes. Julie's a sculptor, and she was applying to art school there."

"Sounds romantic," Bess said, her blue eyes shining. "Did Julie go to Emerson, too?"

Ned shook his head. "Actually, Andrew's four years older than Julie—she's nineteen. They met doing community theater in Melborne. That's where they're both from. It's about ten minutes from here. Andrew was acting, and Julie was painting sets. It was love at first sight."

"If they were so in love, then what was the problem?" she asked Ned.

"Andrew was really torn between Julie and his father, and he kept putting off moving. I think he's really afraid to disobey his father. Mr. Lockwood's a real dragon. Finally Julie just ran out of patience. She decided she'd rather break up with Andrew than wait any longer."

"I feel sorry for Andrew and Julie," Bess said, sighing.

"It *is* too bad," Nancy agreed, "but it could explain what's going on at the inn. Julie might still be so resentful that she's causing trouble just to get back at Andrew and his father."

"It's possible," Ned said. "So that's the story, Bess. I hope you're not too disappointed."

"I'll get over it," Bess said cheerfully. "Besides, I happened to notice that Master Blaster's really cute, too."

A waitress came to take their order, and soon the table was filled with steaming, cheesy enchiladas, crisp tacos, and rice and beans.

As they ate, Nancy kept thinking about Andrew's predicament. "No wonder Andrew kept mentioning how angry his father's going to be," she said aloud, nibbling on her taco. "It sounds as though Mr. Lockwood will have a fit if the inn isn't a success."

"You said it," Ned agreed. "Andrew's petrified. He's almost used up all the money his father gave him for the renovation, and there's still a ton of work to be done. Plasterboard, floors, fixtures. If anything else goes wrong, he'll be a nervous wreck."

"Maybe we can help," Nancy offered. "I mean, if we can figure out who's behind the pranks, that will be one less thing for him to worry about."

Ned was about to object, but then he leaned over to kiss Nancy on the cheek. "So much for taking a break from detecting," he joked. "I bet Andrew *would* appreciate your help."

Tapping the table with her fingernail, Nancy said, "Too bad we can't go back for another look right now. It'd be easier to check out the place without everyone else there, but it's probably locked, right?"

Ned pulled a key from his pocket. "Not to me," he announced. "Andrew gave me this. It's for the back door, so I can get in when he's not there."

After dinner Nancy, Ned, and Bess drove back to the inn and let themselves in the back door. It was the same one Julie had escaped through, Nancy realized. The long hallway was even dark-er than it had been earlier, and Nancy couldn't find a light switch. She fumbled in her purse for her penlight but couldn't find it.

"Uh-oh," Bess said as the three of them felt their way down the pitch-black corridor. "This place is even creepier at night than in the daytime."

At last they reached the door to the ballroom. After quietly opening it, they stepped into the cavernous room, which was already glowing from the shafts of moonlight slanting in through the windows. The dark shadows of sawhorses and ladders made irregular shapes on the floor.

"Aha! Here it is," Nancy crowed, finally finding her penlight in her purse. Flicking it on, she said, "Let's start at the front entrance."

Shining the small, powerful beam, she led the way out of the ballroom and down the main hall. As they stepped into the lobby, she shone her penlight over the sawdust-covered floor, then raised it higher.

Nancy tensed as her beam barely caught a strange swinging movement over their heads.

"What's that?" Bess asked nervously as a faint, creaking noise sounded.

Nancy swept the beam of light toward the ceiling—and her mouth fell open in silent horror.

Hanging from the rafters in a noose was a limp, lifeless body!

Chapter

Three

BESS GAVE A piercing scream. "He's dead!"

Nancy felt stiff with fear, but she forced herself to shine the penlight over the hanging form, from the bottom up.

The person wore no shoes, just white sweat socks and a pair of old, baggy jeans tied tightly around the waist with a rope. Aiming the beam higher, Nancy saw that the torso was covered by a plain gray sweatshirt tucked into the jeans.

Taking a deep breath, she aimed the light at the person's face.

"It's a dummy!" Ned exclaimed as the penlight illuminated a cloth bag filled with soft stuffing.

Nancy felt her whole body slump with relief. "Somebody find a light switch," she said.

A few seconds later some bare bulbs in an overhead fixture went on, casting eerie shadows against the walls. Ned stood by a light switch at the foot of one of the sweeping staircases. Near him Bess was leaning against a ladder, staring in horror at the life-size hanging dummy.

"That beam's too high for someone to reach without a ladder," Nancy pointed out. "Bess, don't move or touch the ladder with your hands. I want to check for fingerprints."

Bess carefully lifted her elbow off the ladder, and Nancy took a closer look. "Hmm, it looks like someone wiped it clean," Nancy said. "There's not a speck on it, but everything else is covered with sawdust."

She cast her eyes downward. "All these footprints are too scuffed to see clearly," she added, frowning. "Whoever hung the dummy went to extra trouble not to leave fingerprints or footprints."

"I don't get it," Ned commented, coming over to the ladder. "If there is a practical joker working here, why would they do something like this? It's not funny at all."

Nancy thought for a moment. "I don't think the person is trying to be funny," she said. "I think they're trying to scare us, or Andrew, or someone else."

"But why?" Bess wondered aloud. "What could they possibly gain by it?"

"Good question," Nancy said. "Let's search the rest of the inn to see if we can figure out an answer."

"What are we looking for?" Bess asked.

"Just keep an eye out for any tools or anything that looks strange," Nancy told her. "But first let's cut this thing down so it won't scare anybody else."

After the dummy had been laid to rest on the dusty floor, Nancy, Ned, and Bess examined the front and back doors. "No sign of forced entry," Nancy observed. "The intruder had to have a key."

Next the three teens searched the downstairs rooms, offices, and hallways. They didn't see anything unusual, or find any of the missing tools, but it was hard to see much in the dim light of the few work lights. A search of the upstairs bedrooms proved equally fruitless.

"The only place we haven't checked is the basement," Nancy said when they returned to the lobby.

"I think it's still locked," Ned told her, "and Andrew has the only key. He doesn't want anyone going down there unsupervised because the stairs are rickety and it's too filled with junk to walk around in."

"Let's try it, anyway," Nancy suggested. "I want to be sure."

Pulling back one of the white drop cloths

THE NANCY DREW FILES

hanging beneath the left staircase, Ned revealed a solid oak door with a rusted knob. He turned the knob and pulled, but it wouldn't budge.

"Oh, well," Nancy said. "We can check again tomorrow, as soon as it's light."

"Good idea," Bess agreed. "Now let's get out of this spooky place before we run into Rosalie Murray's ghost!"

"And that's when we found this," Nancy told Andrew early the next morning, holding up the dummy in the noose to show him. She, Ned, and Bess had arrived before eight so they could talk to Andrew before the TeenWorks crew arrived.

"It was hanging from the rafter up there," Ned added, pointing.

"We thought it was a person," Bess said, putting her hands in the pockets of her pastel pink overalls, which she wore over a matching long-sleeved T-shirt.

Andrew tucked the dummy under his arm and looked anxiously around the empty lobby. "Please don't mention this to anyone else," he said. "If word of this gets out, my work crew might panic, and I can't afford any more delays. I'm going to throw this thing out before anybody sees it."

Nancy followed as Andrew walked to the front door, flung it open, and went outside. The day was so cloudy and overcast that everything seemed to melt into a monotonous dark gray.

"Do you have any idea who might have put the dummy there?" Nancy asked.

Andrew shrugged, then tossed the dummy into a large green Dumpster just outside the entrance. He covered the dummy with some large plastic garbage bags that had been lying on top of the other debris.

"Andrew," Nancy said gently, "I know about Julie. If you think she's out to get you, I wish you'd tell me. The only way I can help you is if you're honest with me."

"It's not Julie," Andrew said, staring at the trees beyond the inn. "I know her. She'd never do something like this."

Nancy couldn't tell if Andrew really believed what he was saying or if he was covering up for Julie. Maybe he still loved her and didn't want her to get in trouble. After all, Andrew hadn't been the one who wanted to break off their engagement.

"Look," he said, turning to face Nancy. His hazel eyes were troubled behind his wire-rimmed glasses. "I appreciate the fact that you're looking into these pranks for me. But lay off Julie, okay?"

"I know you still care about her," Nancy sympathized, "but I can't ignore the facts. Julie was in the inn yesterday, and she ran away from me right after the wailing music was played."

Honk! Honk!

Nancy turned toward the parking lot and saw a

small caravan of cars pull in, followed by the red TeenWorks bus.

Andrew put on a cheerful smile and waved at the teenagers who were piling out of the bus. "Let's just try to forget about all this stuff, okay?" he said to Nancy. "We've got a lot of work to do."

"Hi, Andrew!" Colleen called, stepping out of the bus in a full-length sheepskin coat and striding up the path in brown lizard-skin cowboy boots similar to the black ones she'd worn the day before.

"What's on the agenda for today?" Colleen asked as several of the teenagers gathered around her. Most of them wore jeans, sweatshirts, and sneakers.

"Don't tell me," said Natalia Diaz. "We have to climb on more ladders and do more wiring."

A tall, skinny guy with cornrow braids turned to Andrew. "I guess Natalia never told you that she's afraid of heights."

"Ivan!" Natalia laughed, giving him a playful poke in the ribs.

"We'll be finishing up the wiring today," Andrew said without laughing. "Also, cutting and threading pipes for the bathrooms and the kitchen. Electrical people, talk to Eddie Garcia in the ballroom. Plumbing people, work with Dan Nichols in the dining room. Colleen, Ned, Bess, and Nancy, I'd like to show you guys the basement."

As everyone headed into the lobby, Colleen

remarked, "I thought we'd never see the mysterious basement. Did you finally get a hauler to come pick up all the junk down there, Andrew?"

"Yes, believe it or not," Andrew told her, rolling his eyes. "He'll be here the day after tomorrow, so I want to get everything out and ready for him before then. Anyway, Dan Nichols, our foreman, wants to pour a cement floor Friday, so the area has to be clear."

"Sounds like a tall order. It's already Tuesday," Colleen said as Andrew pulled aside the drop cloth covering the basement door. "We might have to pull some of the kids from their other jobs."

"I hope not," Andrew told her, frowning. "This job's going too slowly as it is." He reached for the key ring that was attached by a metal chain to one of his belt loops and sifted through until he found the key he wanted. Then he unlocked the basement door and pushed it open. A musty, burnt smell wafted upstairs, mixing in with the smell of sawdust.

"Smells like no one's been down there in a long time," Nancy said.

Andrew nodded. "I went down early this morning to connect some work lights," he said, "but I'm the only one who's been in the basement since the fire fifty years ago, not including some inspectors and the architect who measured it for the renovation." Shaking his head, he added, "It's a real mess down there. Most of the stuff is left over from the fire, and half of it's so burned up you can't even tell what it is."

After grabbing a rolled-up blueprint that was leaning against the wall next to the door, Andrew started down the stairs, followed by the others.

"Wow!" Bess exclaimed when they'd gotten halfway down the stairs. "When you said this was a mess, you weren't kidding."

Broken lamps were piled on top of charred wooden beams. Damp, moldy mattresses with the springs sticking out were stacked unevenly, some piles reaching almost to the low ceiling. And there were stacks and stacks of yellowed newspapers and magazines everywhere.

Peering over the mess, Nancy saw that the room stretched for dozens of yards in front of them and to the right and left of the stairs. It seemed to be the same size as the whole first floor. At her feet were the remnants of a wooden floor, but most of it had burned away, leaving bare earth.

"No wonder the inn almost burned down," Colleen commented, picking up a newspaper and glancing at it briefly. "This place is a firetrap. We should get rid of all these newspapers immediately."

"I want to get rid of everything," Andrew said as they all found a place to stand at the foot of the stairs.

Peering out into the basement, Ned said, "So this is going to be a recreation room?"

Andrew unrolled the blueprint he carried and held it out so the others could see. "It's going to be more than that," he said. "There's going to be a dance club, a snack bar, video game room, pool table, and a full-length bowling lane."

Nancy looked over Andrew's shoulder at the neatly drawn blue lines. "Pretty impressive," she told him. "Where do we start?"

"I want to get an inventory of what's down here, see if there's anything salvageable we should keep, and then figure out the best way to get this stuff up the stairs. Some of it's pretty big."

"I think I see a piano," Bess said. "We'll never get that up the stairs."

"We can break up anything that's too heavy," Andrew said. He bent down to pick up a hatchet from beneath the staircase. "I brought a half a dozen of these down for that earlier."

Nancy took a winding path through the broken furniture and other debris. The basement seemed to go on and on, and the damp air still carried the burned-carbon smell of the long-ago fire.

After about twenty steps Nancy found that she couldn't go any farther. Her way was blocked by what looked like a makeshift wall of scraps of lumber, several dressers, and an old metal filing cabinet.

"That's strange," she murmured, veering around the wall. It extended for three sides, with the permanent stone wall closing off the fourth.

"Hey, Andrew!" Nancy called. "Come look at this."

He was still carrying the hatchet when he reached her, followed by Ned, Bess, and Colleen.

"I don't think this was part of the original floor plan," Nancy joked, showing him the makeshift wall.

"And it's not part of the new plan, either," Andrew said. "Let's chop it down. Stand back, everybody."

As Andrew hacked away at the barricade, prying nailed boards, Nancy watched curiously. Someone must have erected it on purpose. But why? And when? Andrew had said the basement had been locked for fifty years.

A ragged opening appeared in the wall, and Andrew stopped so that Nancy could climb through it. It was a tiny space, maybe six feet square. A mattress with a crumpled blanket lumped on it lay on the earth floor beneath a transom window in the stone wall. Around the blanket were greasy wrappers from several fast-food restaurants, a pair of ripped jeans, and a few dirty T-shirts.

"The inn's already had a guest!" Nancy called through the opening to her friends. "And pretty recently, from the looks of it. There's not much dust gathered on this stuff."

"But how could anyone have gotten in here?" Andrew asked, peeking in. "I'm the only one who has a key to the basement, and there's no other way in."

Nancy looked up at the transom window, which was tilted open. "Someone could have fit through there," she said.

"They'd have to be pretty thin," Andrew commented, "but I guess it's possible."

"Maybe this is where Rosalie's ghost goes in her spare time," Bess said with a nervous giggle.

"I doubt it," Ned said, peering through the opening in the makeshift wall. "I've never heard of a ghost who eats Buddy Burgers."

Nancy laughed, climbing back through the opening to rejoin her friends. "My guess is that it was a homeless person. Someone probably found his way up to the lake and spent a few nights here, that's all."

"Or maybe he's still here," Andrew put in. "That could be the explanation we've been looking for. Maybe the guy likes his free room and doesn't want us barging in on him."

"It's possible," Nancy admitted. "But if the person's been wandering around the inn, someone would have been sure to see him by now."

Colleen pressed forward to the opening and scrutinized the small room. "Well, whoever he is, he'll be in for a nasty surprise if he comes back," she said fiercely. "He has no right trespassing. I'll personally supervise the cleanup down here."

"And I'll make sure he doesn't come back,"

Andrew added. "I'll have that window nailed closed right away."

"Yo, Andrew!" called a familiar voice. Nancy heard steps on the stairs. A moment later Blaster appeared at the foot of the stairwell.

"What is it?" Andrew asked irritably.

Nancy noticed that Blaster's face didn't look as cocky and confident as it had yesterday. In fact, he looked seriously worried as he raked a hand over his razor-cut platinum hair.

"Uh-oh," Andrew said. "Don't tell me more tools are missing."

Master Blaster shuffled uncomfortably, kicking the toes of his sneakers against the hard-packed earth. "I think it would be better if I showed you," he finally said. "Natalia Diaz has it, upstairs."

Andrew threaded his way through the basement, pushed past Blaster, and ran up the stairs two at a time. Nancy and the others were right behind him.

"What is it?" Andrew asked breathlessly when they'd all reached the lobby. A group of teenagers stood near the basement door, surrounding a girl with shoulder-length black hair and amber skin. The girl clutched something in her hand.

"Show him, Natalia," Blaster said grimly.

The girl's pretty face was anxious, and her hand trembled as she held out a scrap of paper to Andrew. "I found this upstairs," she said in a faint voice.

Nancy gasped as she looked over Andrew's shoulder and saw the paper. It was splattered with blood and had a message scrawled on it in uneven letters:

The warnings are clear. Stay out of my inn. Leave the past alone, or the walls will come tumbling down!

Chapter

Four

ANDREW READ THE NOTE aloud, then crumpled it in his fist. "This can't be happening," he groaned. "My father will kill me if he sees this."

"Let me look at that again," Nancy said, taking the note from Andrew's hand and smoothing it out. There was something odd about the blood, she realized. It was too thick and bright to be real.

"This looks like nail polish," she murmured, chipping at the glossy red streak with her thumbnail. "Where did you find this, Natalia?"

The dark-haired girl nodded toward the stairs. "I was going into one of the rooms upstairs. It was wedged between the floorboards."

"Was it hard to see?" Nancy asked.

Natalia shook her head no. "It was sticking straight up in the middle of the floor."

Nancy exchanged a meaningful look with Ned and Bess. They'd inspected the upstairs rooms thoroughly last night, and none of them had seen any note. Whoever had left it must have returned to the inn after they'd left or come back early this morning. Or maybe the person had never left, Nancy thought, recalling the hidden room downstairs.

"Can I keep the note?" Nancy asked Andrew. "It might help me figure out what's going on."

"Sure," Andrew said with an unhappy shrug. "I don't want it."

"Mrs. Morgan," Natalia said, approaching Colleen, "I hope you won't think I'm a total wimp, but I'm not sure I want to be part of TeenWorks anymore. This job's getting too dangerous."

"I'm with her," said the tall, lanky boy with cornrow braids. "If the walls come tumbling down, I don't want to be here when it happens."

Colleen gave Andrew a concerned look. "I'm responsible for these kids," she said. "I can't allow them to work in an unsafe environment."

"I understand completely," Andrew said. "I'm just as concerned as you are. But look—so far, no one's been hurt. I think the threats are aimed at the inn itself, not at anybody working here. Bear with me a little while longer, okay?"

"I'll have to leave it up to the kids," Colleen

said. "If any of them want to leave, I can't stop them."

Andrew's shoulders tensed. "Do what you want. But anyone who's working, get back to work."

Nancy noticed some of the kids hesitate, but they all returned to their jobs. The renovation was still in business, at least for the moment. Andrew turned and strode through a small doorway to the right of the lobby.

"Andrew," Nancy called, following him. "Can I talk to you for a minute?"

He stood aside so Nancy could go through the door ahead of him. Nancy entered a small, messy office with stone walls and a desk piled high with papers. A circular file and a phone were balanced precariously on top of some of the papers. A large window looked out onto the driveway.

"Welcome to command central," Andrew said glumly, sitting down behind the desk.

Nancy sat down on a folding chair in front of the desk. "I know you're getting tired of bad news," she told Andrew, "but I have to tell you, this looks even worse than I thought yesterday. This is more than mischief. It looks to me like sabotage. Someone doesn't want you here, and they might not let up until you stop the renovation."

Andrew took off his glasses and wearily rested his head in his hands. "The way things are going, I'd be better off if the inn never opened at all," he mumbled. "All these problems are putting me way over budget. My father's going to think I'm a moron. Maybe I *was* a moron for agreeing to do this project in the first place."

"Stop blaming yourself. Someone else is doing this, not you," Nancy said firmly. "Besides Julie, can you think of anyone else who might have some reason to get back at you or hurt you?"

Andrew lifted his head to look at her, his jaw clenched. "I've already said that Julie didn't do it. She's a sweet, gentle person."

"Who must be pretty angry and hurt right now," Nancy prodded gently.

"Sure she is. And I don't blame her one bit. I'm a wimp for not taking a stand with my father. I deserved for her to leave me," Andrew said miserably. "But Julie's not destructive. I know she's not responsible for what's happening here."

Nancy shot him a skeptical glance. "Then what was she doing at the inn?" she pressed.

With a deep sigh Andrew replied, "I wish I knew. And I wish she hadn't run away so I could tell her again how much I care about her."

Nancy sympathized with him, but she knew that wasn't going to solve his problems. "Is there anyone else who might want to hurt you?"

"No one I can think of," he told her.

"At any rate, I've got two more suspects," Nancy said.

A spark of curiosity lit up Andrew's eyes. "The homeless person?" he guessed.

41

"That's one," Nancy said. "If he's still around, that is. I'm going to go through the stuff downstairs and see if there are any clues to the person's identity."

"Who's the other suspect?" Andrew asked.

"Master Blaster."

Andrew looked at Nancy in surprise. "Really? Why would he want to sabotage me?"

"I don't know," Nancy admitted. "But it was weird that he didn't react yesterday when someone turned off his tape. And he seemed really nervous when I caught him in that back hallway." Getting to her feet, she said, "I'm going to start checking out some of these leads."

"Keep me posted," Andrew said, giving her a weary smile.

Leaving the office, Nancy went looking for Bess. She found her in the dining room, next to the ballroom. It, too, was a cavernous room with a high ceiling and a fireplace that was large enough for a person to stand in. On either side of the fireplace, glass doors led out to a stone patio overlooking the lake. Several sets of sawhorses were scattered throughout the dining room, where teenage workers in goggles were cutting through copper pipes with electric saws.

"Nancy, look!" Bess shouted gleefully from behind a sawhorse. Nancy saw that a tall, balding middle-aged man in overalls was standing behind Bess. "This is Dan Nichols, the construction foreman," Bess went on. "He's showing me how to use a power saw."

"Not bad," Nancy said, grinning as Bess sliced neatly through a pipe.

"Good job," Dan complimented her, then moved on to the group at another sawhorse. When he was out of earshot, Nancy gestured to Bess to turn off the saw.

"Do you think you can handle two jobs at once?" she asked Bess in a low voice. "While you're working, keep an eye on Blaster."

Bess's blue eyes lit up as she said, "You think *he's* the troublemaker?"

"I don't know yet," Nancy said truthfully. "But I think we should watch him. He's probably in the ballroom with the electrical people."

Bess nodded solemnly, but there was a sparkle in her eye. "Then I won't let him out of my sight for a minute."

"I knew I could count on you," Nancy said dryly. "Meanwhile, I'm going to pay Julie Ross a visit."

After grabbing her down jacket from the metal rack in the lobby, Nancy left the inn by the back hallway door. She wanted to cut through the woods Julie had run through the day before to see how far away her store was from the inn.

The day was still dark and overcast, and Nancy had trouble finding her way through the trees. Still, she made a rough guess as to which direction Julie had gone, and soon she could see the cluster of stone buildings that made up the tiny town of Moon Lake.

Within minutes she was standing in front of A Show of Hands, the boutique where Ned had said Julie worked. A bell tinkled as Nancy pushed open the door and went inside. The walls of the store were lined with ceramic bowls, beaded earrings, clay sculptures of birds in flight, and other handmade objects.

In the back a slender girl sat in a separate work area, behind a half-formed piece of wet clay on a clay-spattered table. She wore a white smock over blue jeans, and her hands were covered with the reddish brown clay. As soon as Nancy saw the copper streak in the girl's dark curls, she knew this was the same girl she'd seen the day before.

"May I help you?" the girl asked. Her face, though attractive, looked tired, and there were dark circles under her eyes.

"Just looking," Nancy said lightly. She didn't want to give away her purpose for being at the shop right away. If Julie knew that Nancy was the girl who'd chased her through the woods, she would probably clam up.

"I'm Julie," the girl said with a smile. "If there's anything I can do, just ask."

"Thanks," Nancy said, approaching Julie. "Did you do these bird sculptures?" When Julie nodded, Nancy said sincerely, "They're beautiful. It's hard to believe you can find such high-quality work in an out-of-the-way place like this."

"Tell me about it," Julie said, skillfully shaping the wing of a bird with a flat wooden stick. "I'm from Melborne, but that's almost as small as Moon Lake. Stick the two together, and you'd still need a magnifying glass to find them on a map."

Nancy laughed. "Well, I guess you can leave any time you want, right? Not that you'd want to, of course. It's so peaceful here."

"Peaceful and *boring,*" Julie put in. "As soon as I get into art school, I'm out of here."

"So there's nothing keeping you here, then?" Nancy asked.

Julie focused on her sculpture for a moment, then looked at Nancy with clear gray eyes. "I try not to get tied down to anybody or anything," she said lightly. "Life's easier that way."

"Uh-huh . . ." Nancy pretended to look at a copper candlestick, but she was actually studying Julie out of the corner of her eye. Julie was doing a good job of covering up her hurt feelings. Then again, she didn't know Nancy, so there was no reason for her to reveal anything personal.

"What brings you to Moon Lake?" Julie asked. "It's not exactly the peak of the summer season."

"I'm, uh, helping out at the inn," Nancy said vaguely. "There's a renovation going on."

45

Instantly Julie's eyes grew hard. "I know all about it," she snapped. "Boy, I just can't stand hearing about that old place."

"Why not?" Nancy inquired.

Julie stabbed the clay bird with her wooden stick. "Let's put it this way," she said in an ice-cold voice. "I hope that old dump burns to the ground!"

Chapter

Five

JULIE'S GRAY EYES flashed angrily for a moment. Then, as if she were embarrassed at her outburst, she stared down at her sculpture.

"What do you have against the inn?" Nancy asked.

Julie opened her mouth to answer, but she was interrupted by the tinkling of the bell at the door.

An older woman with fluffy white hair entered and asked, "I'm looking for a rag doll for my granddaughter. Could you show me what you have?"

"I've got to help this customer," Julie told Nancy in a quiet voice. She disappeared through a door in the back, then reemerged a minute later with clean hands and went over to the older woman.

Nancy waited to question Julie, but after the older woman left, a young couple came in. Then a plump middle-aged woman emerged from the back of the store, holding out a cardboard box.

"Julie! Beverly Brandt's order finally came in," the plump woman said. "I want you to deliver it for me."

There was no point in sticking around, Nancy realized. She would have to come back later to question Julie further. Nancy decided to take the road this time, but the walk back to the inn still took only a few minutes. There was no question Julie could come and go quickly.

As Nancy headed up the curved driveway, she saw that a long black limousine with tinted windows was parked right in front of the entrance. The license plate read LOCKWD-1. This had to be Andrew's father's car.

The second Nancy entered the inn, she heard a loud, harsh voice fill the lobby.

"You're a disgrace!" the man's voice yelled. "I trusted you with this job, and what do I find when I get here? Utter chaos!"

"We've had some problems. . . ." Andrew's voice was barely audible.

"Don't give me excuses!" the man yelled. "Give me solutions! If you weren't my son, I'd fire you!"

Nancy wished she weren't overhearing the

conversation. As she quickly crossed the lobby, she glanced into Andrew's office and saw a tall, robust man with steel gray hair slicked straight back. He had a strong profile and was dressed in an expensive-looking charcoal gray suit.

"What's that?" Andrew's father demanded as Andrew mumbled something under his breath.

"Nothing," Andrew said.

Not wanting to embarrass Andrew, Nancy stepped quietly over to the hallway that led to the dining room and ballroom. Behind her she could still hear Mr. Lockwood's angry voice.

"Don't think you're getting out of this," he thundered. "I gave you this job to teach you responsibility. How can I trust you with the rest of my properties if you can't get this right?"

"Maybe if I had a little more money . . ."

"Oh, no," Mr. Lockwood said. "You got yourself into this mess. You'll have to figure a way out on your own."

Shaking her head, Nancy hurried away from the voices. Now that she had seen Mr. Lockwood in action, she understood why Andrew was so scared of him. Anyone would be. She couldn't help feeling sorry for Andrew.

Ahead of Nancy loud rock music was once again blaring from the ballroom. When she got there, she saw that Bess had kept her promise. She wasn't just keeping an eye on Blaster, she was dancing with him!

Blaster was holding Bess's hands and demonstrating some complicated moves while Bess tried to follow. Bess glowed as she gazed at Blaster, while Natalia and several other teens stood nearby, shouting encouragement.

Uh-oh, Nancy thought to herself. Bess wasn't going to be a very objective observer of the deejay. And if he was the person behind all the trouble, Bess might even be in danger.

"Hey!" Andrew shouted, appearing behind Nancy in the door to the ballroom. Apparently, his father had left. "What do you think you're doing?"

Bess guiltily dropped Blaster's hands, and the deejay said, "We're just taking a little break."

"Looks like you're goofing off to me," Andrew said. "Aren't you supposed to be helping Eddie?"

"You got that right!" called a voice from up in the balcony. "Get up here, Blaster. I need you to help me test the master light switch."

Nancy looked up and saw a wiry man in coveralls with straight black hair. Ned was also up in the balcony, removing the rickety-looking guardrail. "Don't get too close to the edge, Eddie," Ned warned. "I haven't put up the new railing yet."

"I'll come help you with that, Ned," Andrew said. He followed Blaster toward the door in the wall that led to the back hall and balcony stairs.

Taking Bess aside, Nancy said in a low voice, "Bess, I need to talk to you about Blaster. I know he's cute—"

"Adorable," Bess cut in, grinning.

"But he may also be very dangerous," Nancy went on.

Bess's eyes turned serious. "I hear what you're saying, Nancy, but I honestly don't think Blaster's guilty. I can feel it."

"I'm not putting down your instincts," Nancy said. "I'm just saying we don't have enough information about him yet to come to any conclusions. So be careful around him, okay?"

Bess didn't look convinced, but she nodded.

"Good," Nancy said. "Now, let's go to the basement. I want to check out the stuff the homeless person left behind."

When they got to the bottom of the stairs, Nancy was amazed at how much cleaner the basement looked than it had earlier. Several wide, clean paths had been cleared through the burnt, broken furniture. Colleen Morgan knelt on the bare earth floor, stacking old newspapers in a cardboard box.

"Are you working here all by yourself?" Nancy asked as she and Bess went over to Colleen.

Colleen looked up and brushed a strand of red hair out of her eyes. "Hmm?" she said distractedly. "Oh, no, not really. I've got some of the kids helping me, but I sent them upstairs for a break. They've been hauling all morning."

"But you're still working," Nancy observed. "That's real dedication."

Colleen barely looked up as she kept going

through the yellowing stacks of newspapers. "I'm just happy to help out."

"Wouldn't you rather be doing something more glamorous than cleaning out a dirty basement?" Bess asked. "I know I would if I were you."

Looking up with a smile, Colleen said, "Believe me, there's nowhere I'd rather be than right here. I've had it easy all my life. Nannies, private school, summers in Europe. Not that I'm complaining, but I *like* working with TeenWorks. It feels good to know I'm making a serious contribution to these kids."

The heavy cardboard box was now full of newspapers, and Colleen lifted it, starting for the stairs.

"Let me help you with that," Nancy offered.

"No, thanks," Colleen said brightly, shifting the box in her arms. "I can handle it."

"Well, at least let us help you clean up the basement," Bess said.

"Don't worry about it," Colleen said over her shoulder. "The kids and I will take care of everything."

Bess stared up the stairs at Colleen's retreating cowboy boots. "Wow. I hope I'm as selfless as she is when I'm a fabulously wealthy socialite someday."

Laughing, Nancy walked down a cleared path toward the spot where she'd found the makeshift room that morning. As she neared the stone wall, she recognized the transom window and the mattress, but all else had been cleared away.

"Oh, no!" Nancy cried, rushing forward. "What happened to my evidence?"

"It was just a bunch of hamburger wrappers," Bess consoled her. "I doubt you could have learned anything from it."

Nancy wanted to kick herself for not thinking to ask Andrew to leave this area alone until she'd examined it.

"Maybe the homeless person's stuff is still here somewhere," Bess said, coming over to join Nancy. "The basement's still pretty messy."

"That's true," Nancy said, brightening. She knelt by the mattress and lifted it up so she could look under it. The only thing she saw was hard-packed earth and a crumpled piece of fabric. Kicking the fabric out with her toe, Nancy let the mattress drop. Then she picked up the moldy-smelling fabric and tried to smooth it out on the ground. It was a T-shirt, filthy and wrinkled, with a few faded words on the front.

"'Bentley High Boneheads, Class of Seventy-seven,'" Bess read, kneeling next to Nancy. There was also a picture of a skull wearing a mortarboard.

Turning the T-shirt over, Nancy saw just two letters printed on the back: G.L.

"I don't get it," Bess said. "What does it mean?"

Shrugging, Nancy said, "We don't even know

if the T-shirt belonged to the person who slept down here. But if it did, the letters on the back could be his initials."

"It looks as if G.L., whoever he is, graduated from Bentley High School in 1977," Bess said.

"That's a good guess," Nancy agreed. "Bentley's not too far from here. We could go over to the high school and try looking him up in one of the yearbooks."

"Sounds good to me," Bess said, standing up and brushing the dirt off her pink overalls.

"I think we've learned everything we can from this," Nancy said, holding her nose as she dropped the T-shirt onto a pile of garbage. "It stinks! Meanwhile, I'm hungry. Have you eaten lunch yet?"

Bess gave her an apologetic look. "We all had sandwiches while you were gone. Let me see if I can scout one out for you, though."

"Thanks," Nancy told her. "I'll check with Ned to see if he wants one, too.

While Bess went off to find sandwiches, Nancy returned to the ballroom. Up in the balcony Andrew and Ned were about to fit the new guardrail into place. Blaster's music filled the room, though Nancy didn't see the deejay anywhere. It was midafternoon, but the day was still so gloomy and overcast that almost no light came in through the windows. The room was lit only by a few work lights scattered around the ballroom.

"Hey, Ned, this is just like Romeo and Juliet," Nancy called, coming directly beneath the balcony.

Ned blew her a kiss as he lifted up the new metal rail, with Andrew directing him.

"'What light through yonder window breaks . . .'" Nancy said, quoting from the play.

"I think you've got it backward," Ned said, grinning down at her. "That's Romeo's line."

"Well, you're the one who's up on the balcony," Nancy said with a laugh.

Ned started to say something, but his voice was suddenly cut off as all the lights went out at once. The ballroom was plunged into dark shadows.

Nancy jumped as a heavy metal object clattered to the floor just inches away from her. A second later she heard a much more frightening sound.

It was the bone-cracking thud of a body landing right beside her, followed by an anguished groan.

Chapter
Six

A FEELING OF DREAD washed over Nancy. "Turn on the lights, somebody!" she yelled.

A moment later the work lights in the ballroom flickered back on, and Nancy saw Ned lying on the floor at her feet, clutching his right arm.

"Ned!" she cried, dropping to her knees beside him. His face had gone white and was contorted in pain. "Did you break your arm?"

Grimacing, Ned nodded. "I think so. You might say my arm broke my fall." He tried to laugh, but then he winced.

"Does anything else hurt?" Nancy asked.

"Not really," Ned answered. He gingerly raised himself to a sitting position and looked around at the group of teens that had crowded around him.

Andrew's head appeared over the edge of the balcony. Blaster was right behind him. "I'll call an ambulance!" Andrew shouted.

"No," Nancy said, pulling her car keys from her purse. "We'll make better time if I drive him to the hospital myself."

"For a guy who fell fifteen feet, you were pretty lucky," Bess said to Ned as Nancy pulled out of the Melborne Community Hospital parking lot a few hours later. "A simple fracture's not too bad."

Ned groaned, sinking against the passenger seat. "Tell that to my coach," he said. His right arm was encased in a plaster cast and held in a sling under his leather jacket. "I won't be able to play basketball for five whole weeks—at the peak of the season."

"I'm just glad you'll be able to play at all," Nancy said.

It was after five o'clock, and the sky was pitch black, starless, and gloomy. *Just the way I'm feeling,* Nancy thought. *It was bad enough that someone was sabotaging the inn, but where did that person come off hurting innocent people?* Nancy was more resolved than ever to track the culprit down and bring him to justice.

"What happened up there, Ned? Did someone push you?" she asked, glancing at her boyfriend.

Ned stared out the window as they passed a strip of used-car lots. "It all went by so fast. All I know is, I was standing close to the edge when the lights went out. I don't think I felt anyone touch me, but I'm not completely sure. I definitely lost my balance."

"So the real question is, who turned out the lights?" Nancy said. "We know Blaster was working up there on the master light switch."

"Yeah, but Eddie was with him," Ned said. "He couldn't have turned out the lights and come forward to push me with Eddie watching."

"Uh, excuse me," said Bess, "but Eddie *wasn't* with Blaster."

Glancing at Bess in the rearview mirror, Nancy asked, "How do you know?"

"Because when I went to the kitchen to look for a sandwich, Eddie was there," Bess said. "He was at the circuit breaker, talking to Blaster over a walkie-talkie. He was telling Blaster to flip certain switches, and then he'd see if the lights were working."

"So what does that mean?" Ned asked. "That Blaster turned off the lights by accident?"

"Maybe," Nancy said, "or maybe he did it on purpose, since no one was watching him."

Nancy turned the Mustang onto the thruway, heading for Mapleton so she could drive Ned home. It was too late to go back to the inn. They'd already called Andrew from the hospital to let him know what was going on.

"It's possible Julie paid the inn another visit," Nancy added. "Though I'm not sure how she could have turned off the lights with Blaster in the alcove by the switches."

"Anyway, why would she do that?" Ned asked. "She was mad at Andrew, not me."

"That might have been the real accident," Bess put in. "Maybe Julie intended to push Andrew off the balcony but couldn't see in the dark and pushed you instead."

Shaking his head doubtfully, Ned said, "I don't know, Julie's not like that. She's sweet."

"Andrew said the same thing, but she didn't sound so sweet when I talked to her at the crafts store today," Nancy said. She quickly recounted Julie's bitter remarks about the inn.

Ned still didn't look convinced. "There has to be some other explanation for what happened," he said. "Maybe it was the person hiding in the basement. He could still be around somewhere, too."

"Nothing points to him being behind any of these accidents," Nancy told him, "but I do want to get over to Bentley High School and see if I can find out anything about the Boneheads and G.L."

"What are you doing here?" Andrew exclaimed Wednesday morning as Nancy, Ned, and Bess entered the inn's lobby. Andrew was on his way out the door, a ledger under his arm and car keys jangling in his hand. "You should be home taking care of that arm, Ned."

Grinning, Ned said, "I figured even if I can't work, you could use some moral support after everything that's happened."

"That's for sure," Andrew said glumly. "We had another incident last night."

"Oh, no!" Bess said with a gasp. "Was anyone else hurt?"

Andrew shook his head. "Fortunately not. I'm on my way to meet my father at his office, but I guess I can take a minute to show you." He crossed the lobby and went inside his office, reappearing a moment later with a note in his hand. The words *Come back to me* were printed on it, and bloodred paint drippings covered the page.

Taking the other message out of her purse, Nancy compared it to the one Andrew held. The handwriting in both notes looked the same, and so did the red enamel paint.

"'Come back to me?'" Bess repeated. "I don't get it. Who's 'me'? And who is 'me' talking to?"

Nancy frowned and turned to Andrew. "You're not going to want to hear this," she told him, "but that message could be from Julie. Maybe it's her way of saying she wants to get back together."

For the first time since Nancy had mentioned Julie as a suspect, Andrew didn't object. "It's possible," he admitted quietly. "But I have no idea how she could have gotten inside the inn. All the doors are locked at night, and there's no way she could get a key."

"The message could also be from the ghost that's still haunting the inn, looking for her lover," Bess piped up.

Andrew looked at his watch and groaned. "I don't have time for this now. My father wants me to give him a full accounting of all the work we've done. I'd better leave now or I'll be late."

After Andrew left with his ledger, Nancy, Ned, and Bess headed for the ballroom, where they found Dan Nichols and about ten of the TeenWorkers nailing thick gray slabs of plasterboard to the wooden framework against the walls. The clattering and banging of their hammers was nearly drowned out by loud, fifties-style rock and roll blaring from the stereo on the balcony.

"Ned, would you come up to the balcony with me?" Nancy asked. "I want to try to figure out what happened yesterday."

"Might as well," Ned agreed, with a nod at his cast. "I'm not going to be much use here."

They climbed the back stairs to the balcony, and Nancy shone her penlight into the dimly lit alcove right outside the entrance to the balcony. The master light switch was there, now fully wired with eight black dials.

"This must have been where Blaster was working yesterday," Nancy said. "It's only a few feet from the alcove to the front of the balcony, where you were working. He definitely could have turned off the lights and pushed you."

"I'm still not sure I was pushed," Ned said.

"But we *are* sure someone turned out the lights," Nancy reminded him. She stepped through the open doorway and onto the balcony. There was a second light switch just inside the door.

"This controls the lights downstairs, too," Nancy said after quickly flipping the switch off and on.

She thought for a moment, then said excitedly, "That means Julie *could* have turned off the lights. It's possible that she sneaked up the stairs past the alcove where Blaster was working. She wouldn't have needed to use the master switch. She could have turned the lights out from here."

"Maybe," Ned said. Nancy was glad that he kept a careful distance from the balcony's edge, even though the new railing had been installed.

"Now that I think about it," Nancy went on, "Julie was sent on an errand by her boss yesterday, not long before your accident. It would have been a perfect opportunity for her to come here without her boss wondering where she was."

As Nancy peered at the balcony switch, she noticed a reddish brown muddy substance on the lever. "Hey, Ned," she called. "Look at this."

He came over and picked at the dried, cakey substance with his good hand. "Looks like clay."

"And it matches the color of the clay Julie was working with yesterday," Nancy said excitedly. After searching in her purse for a slip of paper, she chipped off a sample of the reddish brown substance and carefully folded it inside.

"Now I'd really better pay Julie another visit at the store," Nancy said, "so I can check this sample against the clay she uses. I'm almost positive it'll be a match."

Nodding, Ned said, "I think I remember Andrew saying she doesn't work there every day, though. Maybe you can get her home address from Andrew. He has a file of address cards in his office."

"Good idea," Nancy said. "While I'm at it, I'd like to get Blaster's address, too. Do you think Andrew would mind if I looked them up now? I wouldn't disturb anything."

"That should be okay," Ned told her. "It's not top secret information or anything."

Nancy and Ned went back down the balcony stairs, through the ballroom, and down the hallway to Andrew's office, off the lobby. After knocking softly, Nancy pushed open the door. Hearing a jangling sound, she checked behind the door and found two keys hanging from hooks. One was labeled Front Door and the other said Back Door.

"So that's how the intruder got in at night," Nancy murmured, half to herself.

Giving Nancy a perplexed look, Ned asked, "What are you talking about, Nan?"

She showed Ned the keys. "There are plenty of times when Andrew's not in the office," she said. "Anyone could have come in here and borrowed the keys, then made copies and returned the originals before Andrew noticed they were gone."

"That's definitely possible," Ned agreed.

Moving over to the desk, Nancy found a circular file of address cards precariously balanced next to the phone on top a pile of papers. She pulled a notebook from her purse and jotted down Blaster's and Julie's addresses.

"They both live in Melborne," Nancy said. "That will save time if we need to visit them at home. . . . Oops!"

Nancy reached out to steady the circular file, which had started to slide down the stack of papers. She pushed some of the papers aside so she could set the file down on the desk. As she did, a bright red ink stamp on several of the papers caught her eye.

" 'Overdue,' " she read aloud, then peered more closely at the papers. "These are bills. Electrical cable, five hundred dollars," she read off one. "Copper pipes, seven *thousand* dollars."

Shuffling through the papers, Nancy saw that every single one of them was a bill, and they were all overdue.

Nancy did some quick mental calculations.

"These run into tens of thousands of dollars!" she exclaimed.

Looking over her shoulder, Ned observed, "Andrew wasn't exaggerating when he said he was in debt."

"And his debt is even worse than we realized," Nancy said. She pressed her lips together, concentrating as an idea began to form in her mind. "Maybe Andrew wasn't joking when he said he'd be better off if the inn never opened," she said slowly.

"What are you saying, Nan?" Ned asked.

Nancy paused, gathering her thoughts. "You've said Andrew's always been afraid to stand up to his father," she said at last. "Maybe Andrew was causing all the problems because he didn't want responsibility for the inn and couldn't figure any other way out."

Ned's mouth fell open. "You mean . . ."

Nancy nodded. "Maybe the person sabotaging the inn is Andrew himself!"

Chapter

Seven

NANCY GASPED as she realized something else, so horrible she could hardly even think about it.

"Andrew was the person closest to you when the lights went out," she said softly to Ned. "He would have had the best opportunity to turn off the lights and push you off the balcony."

"No way!" Ned protested vehemently. "Andrew would never do anything to hurt me. Besides, why would he do something like that?" he asked. "Hurting me won't save the inn."

"Maybe he doesn't want to save it," Nancy said. "If he's really desperate to get out of his father's clutches, he might do anything, even hurt you, to stop the renovation. He could have caused all these accidents and written the threatening notes so that it would seem like it wasn't his fault that he failed."

Ned shook his head. "That's not like Andrew," he insisted. "He's not the bravest person in the world, but he's not a liar."

"He's not a renovator, either," Nancy reminded him. "He wants to be an actor, right? You admitted that he's only working for his father because he's too scared to say no."

Ned's expression darkened, and he turned away from Nancy, slowly leaving the office.

"I know it's upsetting," Nancy said, following him into the lobby. "But think about it. Most of the damage was done at night. Andrew could have stayed late, after everyone left, and written the notes or rigged up the dummy."

Turning to meet Nancy's gaze, Ned said, "But what about the ghost noises coming from the stereo?" Ned asked. "Andrew was standing in the ballroom with us when that happened."

"He could have used a remote control," Nancy suggested.

"But we didn't find a tape or anything in the stereo with ghost noises on it," Ned said. "Andrew couldn't have removed it because we were with him the whole time."

Ned had a point, Nancy realized. "But if he's working with someone—"

"I'm glad *someone's* working."

Nancy jumped at the sound of Andrew's voice behind her and Ned. Whirling around, she saw that Andrew was just coming in the front entrance, his ledger under his arm.

"Who are we talking about?" Andrew asked.

"Um, my father," Nancy quickly lied. "He's just hired a new partner at his law firm."

Shooting Nancy a hard look, Ned walked quickly over to Andrew and put his left arm around his friend. "How'd it go with your dad?" he asked.

Before Andrew could answer, Colleen appeared between the marble columns framing the front hallway. "Do you guys have a minute?" she asked. "I'm calling a little powwow in the ballroom."

"Right now?" Andrew asked, grimacing. "I don't think we can spare the time. My dad says if we don't pick up the pace, he might have to fire TeenWorks and get a professional contractor."

Colleen drew herself up straighter. "My kids are very professional," she said in a defensive tone. "You'll be lucky if we stay on the job after all that's happened here. That's why I'd like to have a meeting with you, as a matter of fact."

The tension in the room was so thick that Nancy felt she could cut it with a knife. No one said a word as Colleen led the way into the ballroom. About fifteen people, including Bess, sat on the floor, eating sandwiches and drinking cans of soda.

"Well?" Andrew asked, crossing his arms.

"I'm concerned," Colleen began. "There've been too many accidents on this job. I just don't feel comfortable having these kids in danger. We can't risk another fall like the one that happened yesterday." She nodded toward Ned's fractured arm. "That's why I think this renovation should be called off, at least until we figure out who's responsible for all the problems here."

Andrew quickly scanned the teenagers' faces. "I'm concerned about everyone's safety, too," he said. "But I can't afford to stop the renovation. We've lost too much time and money as it is."

"It's too dangerous to continue," Colleen insisted.

Natalia Diaz spoke up from where she was sitting cross-legged on the floor. "It's more than dangerous. It's depressing," she said. "We've worked so hard here, but lots of the stuff just gets undone."

"Hey," Colleen said, going over to hug Natalia. "Your moods are upsetting me even more than all the accidents. Cheer up, guys!"

The teenagers looked at one another. After an uncomfortable silence, Colleen clapped her hands and strode back and forth in front of the group. "I know the perfect thing to get us all out of this slump," she said, her green eyes sparkling. "Let's have a party!"

"Now?" Master Blaster asked hopefully.

Colleen laughed. "I was thinking about after

69

work hours—like, how about tomorrow night? We can have it at my house. I'll call a caterer, and Blaster can provide the music, of course. If you all show up, it'll be a big bash."

A round of cheers echoed in the ballroom, and Andrew looked expectantly at the teenagers. "So? Does that mean we can get back to work?"

"For now," Colleen said. "But if there's any more trouble, you'll be hearing from me."

"Fine," Andrew said with a resigned sigh. "Meanwhile, lunchtime's over, folks. Everybody back to work."

As the group broke up, Bess got to her feet and came over to Nancy. "I guess I'd better keep an eye on Blaster," she whispered cheerfully, watching the deejay as he headed into the hallway.

"This time I'm coming with you," Nancy said firmly. "I want to find out what he knows about Ned's fall from the balcony."

The two girls followed Blaster into the hall, past the dining room, to the last room on the left. Like the bathrooms upstairs, this room was bare, with pipes sticking out of the framework walls in a few places.

"Can we help, Blaster?" Bess asked, pushing up the sleeves of the yellow sweatshirt she wore over her jeans.

Master Blaster grinned when he saw Bess. "Do you know anything about electricity?" he asked.

"Not really," Bess admitted.

"That's funny," Blaster said, moving a step

70

closer to Bess. "Because as soon as you walked into the room, I felt a power surge."

Bess's face turned red, and her eyes sparkled with pleasure. Obviously, Nancy was going to have to keep an eye on *both* of them!

"What are you working on?" Nancy asked as the deejay knelt on the floor by a tool chest and pulled out a pair of metal clippers. He deftly sliced through a heavy electrical cable attached to the wooden wall frame and pulled out a black and a white wire.

"I'm wiring some outlets," he said, taking a rectangular metal box from his tool chest. Swiftly and efficiently he ran the wires through a hole in the top of the box and clamped the metal box to the drywall stud.

"Pretty impressive," Nancy said as she watched.

Master Blaster shrugged. "It's a living."

"You don't sound too excited about working here," Nancy said. "Or maybe it's just all the strange things that have been happening."

"It's just that I won't be working here for too long, that's all," Blaster said.

Before Nancy could probe further, Bess said, "It's just until you become a top deejay and record producer." Turning to Nancy, she said, "Blaster's told me all about his music."

"It's very fresh," Blaster said. "Sort of a mix of my own melodies and lyrics over existing music and sound effects. It's hard to explain."

"It sounds really original," Bess said. She seemed to have totally forgotten about the case.

With a stern look at her friend, Nancy said to Master Blaster, "It must have been pretty weird yesterday, up in the balcony, when all the lights went out. What happened? Did you flip the dining room switch by accident?"

Blaster's cocky demeanor vanished instantly. His face reddened, and his hands shook a little. "I swear I didn't do it," he said. "I was running a check on the downstairs lights when it happened. Eddie can back me up."

Master Blaster seemed awfully nervous for someone who claimed to be innocent. "I guess the person who did it must have run right past you, then," Nancy said. "Did you hear or see anything strange while you were working up there?"

Blaster shook his head, then suddenly became very intent on screwing the metal plate into the wall. "I didn't see anything," he said hesitantly. "I had my back to the stairs and my ear to the walkie-talkie."

Nancy felt certain that he was lying. She was about to press him for more information when Andrew poked his head in through the doorway.

"Can you give me a hand, Blaster?" Andrew asked. "I need some help in the ballroom."

"Sure," Blaster said, standing up quickly. He looked relieved to have an excuse to leave.

Shrugging at each other, Nancy and Bess followed the guys back into the ballroom. Andrew went over to stand beside a pulley that was attached by a cable to the old crystal chandelier hanging from the ceiling. Ned, Colleen, and half a dozen other teenagers were gathered nearby.

"It's time to take this baby down," Andrew said. "It's been up since 1913, but it's damaged beyond repair."

"Too bad," Nancy said, admiring the grand chandelier.

Andrew placed both hands on the pulley's winding mechanism. "I need you and Ivan to help me crank this, Blaster," he said.

The deejay stood beside Andrew and the boy with cornrow braids. With all their strength they turned the crank. Nancy saw beads of sweat break out on the three guys' foreheads as they began to slowly lower the chandelier.

"That thing must weigh a ton," she commented.

"It's so sad," Bess said. She moved toward the chandelier and craned her neck so she could see it. "It's kind of like the end of an era."

"Hey, Bess," Nancy began with a worried glance toward where Andrew, Master Blaster, and Ivan strained against the crank. "I don't think it's a good idea to stand—"

The sudden sound of tinkling glass overhead drowned out Nancy's warning. Looking up, she felt her breath catch in her throat. The cable had ripped almost in two, and the chandelier was swinging crazily.

The next thing Nancy knew, there was a ripping noise and the chandelier was hurtling down through the air, straight toward Bess's head!

Chapter
Eight

NANCY LEAPT FORWARD, throwing her weight against Bess and knocking them both out of the way. A split second later the chandelier landed with a deafening crash against the floor.

For a moment the two of them lay motionless, stunned and breathing heavily. Thousands of shards of broken crystal surrounded them. Worried cries rang out in the room, and she and Bess were soon surrounded by Ned, Andrew, and the others.

"Are you okay?" Ned asked, his brown eyes filled with concern.

Nancy sat up gingerly. "I think so," she said. "Bess?"

"S-still in one piece," Bess said in a squeaky voice. With Blaster's help, she rose to her feet. "Thanks, Nancy. That's probably the zillionth time you saved my life, but it means just as much every time."

Looking gravely from Nancy to Bess, Andrew said, "Maybe Colleen's right. This job *is* getting too dangerous. If people's lives are in danger—"

"We're fine," Nancy assured him, taking Ned's hand as he helped her up.

"But who knows what's going to happen next?" Andrew said, shaking his head. "I just increased my insurance coverage, but I don't think it's going to be enough if these accidents keep up."

Hearing Andrew's words, something clicked in Nancy's mind. Insurance! she thought excitedly. That could be the whole key to what was happening.

Maybe Andrew had decided to junk the whole project and collect on his insurance, Nancy thought. He could blame the inn's failure on the saboteur, and he'd be able to get back some of his father's investment. That way he'd be free to go to California and pursue his acting career, and no one would ever have to know that he was the one causing the accidents in the first place.

Nancy was almost sure that foul play was behind this incident, too. She bent over the huge pile of shattered crystal and stared at the broken end of thick cable that was attached to a metal ring at the top of the chandelier.

Hmm, that's strange, she thought. The cable end wasn't torn evenly. Half of it was neatly cut, as if someone had sliced through it on purpose with metal clippers.

Nancy took Andrew aside as Bess, Colleen, and some of the teens found brooms and started sweeping up the crystal shards. "I think someone cut halfway through this cable," Nancy told him, "knowing that the weight of the chandelier would break it the rest of the way."

"But that's impossible," Andrew insisted. "I checked the cable last night, and it was fine."

"You weren't around for a while this morning, though," Nancy countered. "Someone could have sliced it then." *If you didn't do it yourself,* she added silently.

Andrew shook his head. "I don't see how," he said. "The pulley and cable were locked in a closet in my office all night. I just brought it out myself a few minutes ago."

Speaking in a low voice, Nancy told Andrew her theory that someone might have sneaked into the office and copied the keys when he wasn't there. "It could have been Blaster, or the homeless person," Nancy said. "Or maybe Julie."

Andrew started to object, but Nancy cut him off. "Whoever it is, they might be planning to return tonight to plant more nasty surprises."

Her blue eyes sparkled as she added, "I have an idea, though." Gesturing for Ned and Bess to join them, she said, "Why don't we camp out here tonight? Or maybe I should say camp in. If someone tries to break in, we'll have a better chance of catching them off guard."

"Sounds like fun," Bess said. "But after this narrow escape, I think I'm going to need a big picnic dinner to revive my spirits."

"That can be arranged," Ned said, smiling.

Nancy wondered if Andrew would try to resist the sleepover, but all he said was, "I could bring some sleeping bags. We have tons of camping stuff in our attic at home. My family used to go camping a lot when I was a kid."

"You can stay up all night and tell ghost stories," Master Blaster said from where he was sweeping crystal shards nearby.

Nancy wished she'd been more careful to make sure no one overheard their plans. Colleen seemed to have heard them talking, too, because she walked over to Nancy a moment later.

"I know I'm not responsible for you the way I am for the other kids," Colleen said, "but are you sure staying here's a good idea? You could be dealing with a very dangerous person."

"We'll be fine," Ned assured her. "There are four of us. You know what they say about safety in numbers."

Colleen looked skeptical. "But what if something happens to you? You're miles from the nearest police station."

"Thanks for worrying about us," Nancy said, "but we've been through a lot together. We've gotten pretty good at taking care of ourselves."

With a shrug Colleen said, "Suit yourselves." Stepping away, she called out, "Come on, TeenWorks people! Anyone who's not sweeping, let's get back to the basement. We have to clean out the rest of the stuff by tomorrow night."

As most of the teens followed Colleen out the ballroom door, Nancy turned to Andrew again.

"Would you mind if I borrowed Ned for the rest of the afternoon? I've got a little checking up I want to do," she said. "We can pick up some food for dinner and meet you back here tonight for our camp-out."

"Sure, if it will help you find whoever's doing all this stuff," Andrew said. "See you guys later."

"Where are we going?" Ned asked when they got to the lobby.

Nancy draped his leather jacket over his bad arm, then slipped on her down parka. "I thought this would be the perfect excuse to spend some time alone with you," she said, grinning. "If we have to spend your vacation chasing after suspects, at least we can do it together."

"There's no one I'd rather chase suspects with," Ned said with a warm look that made Nancy tingle all over. "Who's first on our list?"

"I want to find out if the clay sample from the balcony matches the clay Julie works with," Nancy said. "Then I want to go to Blaster's house and see if I can figure out what he's hiding."

She and Ned got in the Mustang, and Nancy headed for the small road that curved around the lake and into the town of Moon Lake. As she approached A Show of Hands, Nancy saw that Julie and the middle-aged woman were just locking up the boutique.

"Hmm," Ned said as Julie got into an old gray car and pulled away from the curb. "I guess you'll have to wait to check out that clay sample."

Nancy slowed down, keeping a discreet distance behind Julie's car. "I'm going to follow her," she decided.

After a short drive down curving, tree-lined roads, Nancy followed Julie's car into a suburban neighborhood.

"This is Melborne," Ned said, reading a sign. "She's probably going home."

A few minutes later Julie turned onto a quiet street and pulled up alongside a small but well-kept white house.

"Not too incriminating so far," Ned said.

"No," Nancy agreed. She parked diagonally across the street and watched as Julie got out of her car and headed up the front walk. After Julie had closed the front door behind her, Nancy said, "I'm going to try to talk to her."

Ned nodded. "I'd better stay here. Julie knows

I'm Andrew's friend. If she sees me with you, she might not be too cooperative."

"Good point," Nancy said, opening her door. "I'll try not to be too long."

After hurrying up the front walk, Nancy rang Julie's doorbell and waited. Half a minute later Julie opened the door. She looked even more tired than the day before, and her brown curly hair looked messy and unkempt. Nancy wondered if Julie had slept well the night before—or if she'd been busy sabotaging the cable at the inn.

Julie looked at Nancy in surprise. "Weren't you in my store yesterday?" she asked.

Nancy nodded, then said, "I know you're probably surprised to see me. I'm Nancy Drew."

"That name sounds familiar for some reason." Julie said, her gray eyes growing hazy.

"Could I talk to you for a minute? I'd like to ask you a couple of questions."

"That's it," Julie said, snapping her fingers. "I've heard Ned Nickerson talk about you. You're a detective, right?"

There was no point denying it. "Yes, but—"

"Did Andrew's father send you here?" Julie asked suspiciously.

"No," Nancy said quickly. "Mr. Lockwood has nothing to do with this."

"I don't believe you," Julie retorted, scowling. "He's already had one private detective tailing me. Isn't that man ever satisfied? He's totally ruined my life."

81

Julie slammed the door in Nancy's face, and Nancy heard the sound of a deadbolt locking.

"Please, Julie!" Nancy called, knocking on the door. "You've got it all wrong. . . ."

A few seconds later Nancy heard a stereo blasting loud rock music and saw the window shades being yanked down. Julie had made it very clear that she wasn't home—at least not for Nancy.

"What happened?" Ned asked when Nancy got back in the car.

"She wouldn't even talk to me," Nancy said, buckling her seat belt. "She thinks I'm working for Andrew's father."

"So what do we do now?" Ned asked.

"Let's find Blaster's house," Nancy said. She flipped open her notebook to find the address. "I know he lives in Melborne, too. Here it is— Eighteen Rose Avenue. Maybe we could find a gas station."

Ned's eyebrows knit together, and he said, "I thought we passed the street not far back. Why don't we turn around?"

Nancy made a U-turn, then headed the Mustang back the way they had come. After only a few blocks, she saw Rose Avenue off to the right. She turned onto it and drove several blocks until she came upon number eighteen, a two-story brick house.

Together, Nancy and Ned walked up to the front steps, and Nancy tapped on the iron door knocker. A few moments later the door opened a crack, and an elderly woman peeped out at them. She wasn't very tall, but she was heavyset, with short, steel gray hair.

"Yes?" the woman asked.

"Hi, I'm Nancy Drew," Nancy said pleasantly. "And this is Ned Nickerson. We're working with Blaster on the renovation of the Lakeside Inn."

"Has something happened to him?" the old woman asked, her dark eyes fearful. "He said there'd been some accidents the past few days."

"No, no, nothing like that," Nancy said quickly. "Blaster's fine. But we are trying to figure out who's been causing the accidents there, and we were wondering if we could talk to you."

"Me?" the old woman asked, opening the door a little wider. "You don't think my grandson's responsible, do you? He's a good boy."

"Blaster's your grandson?" Ned asked.

The old woman nodded. "He's lived with me since his parents died, ten years ago."

"Oh, I'm very sorry," Nancy said gently. "We don't know for sure who's responsible for what's happening at the inn," she added. "But you might be able to help us rule out Blaster."

The woman peered from Nancy to Ned to Ned's cast. After a long moment she said. "Please, come in. I'm Olivia Deekman."

Mrs. Deekman showed them into a small living room furnished with heavy, dark wooden furniture. A fire crackled in a fireplace against one wall, and dozens of framed photographs rested on the mantel. Nancy and Ned sat down on a green square-backed sofa as Blaster's grandmother settled in an armchair by the fireplace.

"What would you like to know?" Mrs. Deekman asked.

Nancy pulled from her purse the threatening note Natalia Diaz had found and held it out to Mrs. Deekman. "Does this look like Blaster's handwriting?" she asked.

Blaster's grandmother took the note and studied it, then shook her head. When Nancy asked her if she knew whether Blaster had any red enamel paint, the old woman said, "All he's got upstairs is a bunch of electronic equipment."

"What about tools? Have you noticed any new ones in his room, like a soldering iron, drill bits, anything like that?" Ned asked, naming the items that had been taken from the inn.

The old woman shook her head again. "Hubert's got a pretty complete set already. He hasn't bought anything new in—"

"Hubert?" Ned repeated, his mouth falling open. "Is that his real name?"

The old woman lifted a hand to her mouth. "Oh, my. Hub— Blaster's going to be mad at me that I let it slip. He hates for people to find out. He's terribly embarrassed about it. I don't know why. It's a perfectly respectable name. He was named after my father."

"Why did he change it?" Nancy asked, although she thought she knew the answer. The name didn't fit his cool image at all.

Mrs. Deekman sighed and stared into the fire. "In the past year and a half Hubert's changed drastically—and more than just his name. His looks, his personality, everything."

Blaster's grandmother got up from her chair and walked over to the mantel, murmuring, "I think I have an old picture here somewhere." She ran her finger lightly along the tops of the framed photographs until she found what she was looking for. "Here it is," she announced.

Mrs. Deekman handed Nancy a silver-framed color photograph of her grandson, and Nancy stared at it in stunned silence.

"Hubert looked a lot different back then, didn't he?" Mrs. Deekman said.

That was the understatement of the year, Nancy thought. Master Blaster did indeed look different. The photograph showed a scrawny kid with dark brown hair, owlish glasses, and a jacket that looked two sizes too big.

"I think the change started when his old girl-friend broke up with him," Mrs. Deekman went on. "Hubert was devastated. I think he was hoping that if he changed his image, he'd win her back."

Nancy looked curiously at the older woman. "Did the plan work?" she asked.

Mrs. Deekman shook her head no. "Poor Hubert."

"He must really have been in love with her for him to change his whole look and personality," Ned said. "Who was she?"

"Her name was Julie," Mrs. Deekman said. "Julie Ross."

Chapter

Nine

Nancy's mind was reeling. Master Blaster's ex-girlfriend was Andrew's former fiancée!

That opened up a whole new realm of possibilities in the case. Could Blaster and Julie be working together to ruin Andrew's inn project? That would explain what Blaster was doing by the back door the day Julie had run off through the woods.

"Tell me about Julie," Nancy said to Mrs. Deekman. "Why did she and Blaster break up?"

Mrs. Deekman replaced the picture on the mantel and sat back down in her armchair. "Hubert and Julie have been friends since they were children," she explained. "They dated in

87

high school, until Julie broke up with him the summer after their junior year."

Ned prodded Nancy in the ribs with his cast, then asked Mrs. Deekman, "What happened? Did she meet someone else?"

Blaster's grandmother nodded sadly. "Julie met an older fellow, a college student," she said. "It was a whirlwind romance, from what I hear. Hubert couldn't accept the fact that Julie didn't love him anymore. He was very jealous."

"And that's when he changed his image?" Nancy guessed.

Mrs. Deekman nodded. "Hubert was always interested in music. When Julie left him, he swore to become a rich and famous recording star, just so she'd regret that she'd walked away from him."

"He certainly seems very ambitious," Nancy said. "I guess that's helped him get over Julie."

"Oh, no," Mrs. Deekman disagreed. "He's never forgotten her. In fact, when she broke up with the college fellow a few weeks ago, Hubert tried to win her back."

"How does Julie feel about Blaster now?" Nancy asked. "Does she want to get back together with him?"

"No. Julie's still pining over her ex-fiancé. Poor Hubert."

Mrs. Deekman probably didn't realize it, but she'd just provided Nancy with a motive linking Blaster to the crimes at the inn: revenge. He might be trying to get back at Andrew for stealing Julie away from him.

Getting to her feet, Nancy said, "Thank you for all your help, Mrs. Deekman." Ned rose, too, and Mrs. Deekman showed them to the door and said goodbye.

Nancy waited until she and Ned were in the car and halfway down the block before she said, "Can you believe it? Blaster and Julie? I never would have guessed it."

"You've got everything you need, now, huh?" Ned said. "Blaster had the motive to get back at Andrew, and he definitely seemed nervous and edgy the past few days. If we can prove he copied the keys or catch him tonight, we'll have it all wrapped up. I told you it wasn't Andrew."

Although it was only five-thirty, it was already dark outside. Nancy peered at the street signs lit up by her headlights, retracing her way back to the inn. "I agree that Blaster is our number-one suspect," she said, "but I think it's a little premature to convict him. There are too many other things we can't explain."

"Like what?" Ned asked.

"Julie's visits to the inn, for one thing," Nancy said. "We know she's been there, but apparently it hasn't been to visit Blaster."

Turning onto the little road that led to Moon Lake, she added, "I can't rule out Andrew, either. He seems to have more reason to want the inn to fail than to succeed. And then there's the uninvited guest in the basement. I still have to follow up on that T-shirt I found down there."

Ned leaned forward to turn up the heat, taking care not to hit his cast against the dashboard. "Well, I'm still convinced it's Master Blaster, but I guess we'll learn more tonight."

Andrew and Bess were in the ballroom unrolling sleeping bags when Ned and Nancy got back to the inn. The big room was dark except for a circle of work lights around the sleeping bags.

"Great, you're back. And you remembered dinner!" Bess called, gesturing to the shopping bag Ned carried.

"We stopped at the store in Moon Lake," he explained, putting the bag down.

Nancy squinted dubiously up at the lights. "We'd better turn those out," she said. "We don't want to scare away the intruder. We should check the front and back doors, too, to make sure they're locked. That way we'll have a little time to hide if we hear the intruder."

"I'll be right back," Andrew said. He jogged across the ballroom toward the main hall, returned after a minute, then disappeared through the door under the balcony.

"We're all set," he said when he came back. He turned out the work lights one by one until the vast ballroom was lit only by silvery moonlight. It took a few minutes for Nancy's eyes to adjust to the darkness, but soon she could make out her friends' faces fairly well.

"So what did you find out?" Bess asked, unloading the grocery bag as Nancy and Ned sat down side by side on a sleeping bag.

Nancy filled them in on how they'd followed Julie and on Mrs. Deekman's revelation about Julie and Blaster.

"Master Blaster and Julie?" Andrew asked, an expression of total shock on his face. "She said she'd had a boyfriend, but I never would have guessed it was him."

"Well, it was. Working here could give him the perfect chance to pay you back for stealing Julie away," Nancy told Andrew.

Even in the darkness Nancy could see the troubled look in Bess's eyes. Nancy decided to let the subject drop for now, but over the next few hours she noticed that Bess was quieter than usual and only nibbled at her roast beef sandwich and potato salad.

"So what's the plan, Nancy?" Ned asked after they'd cleaned up after dinner.

Nancy thought for a moment. "I guess we should stay here," she said. "If someone comes in the back door, they'll have to walk through here, and we're close enough to the front door to hear if someone comes in through the lobby."

"What about sleeping?" Bess asked.

"We can take turns keeping watch," Nancy

said. She planned to stay awake the whole time, though, so she could keep an eye on Andrew. He might try to sneak away during his watch, while the rest of them were asleep.

Bess yawned. "I'm tired already," she said. "What time is it?"

"Almost ten o'clock," Nancy said, checking her watch.

"This is sort of romantic, isn't it?" Ned asked, moving closer to Nancy and putting his left arm around her.

"Romantic wasn't the word *I* was thinking of," came Bess's nervous voice.

"You're not still worried about the ghost, are you?" Ned asked her.

Bess smiled sheepishly. "I know it's silly, but in the dark, I feel like Rosalie's ghost could be right here in this room."

Grinning at her friend, Nancy said mischievously, "Maybe her ghost *is* here."

"Yeah, right," Ned said sarcastically. "And maybe I'm—"

He broke off as a sudden, frigid blast of cold air washed over them. A moment later Nancy heard loud, shuffling footsteps echoing somewhere overhead.

"It's Rosalie's ghost," Bess whispered hoarsely, sitting bolt upright.

Nancy craned her neck, looking in the direction the sound was coming from. She tried to stay calm, but she could feel the hairs rise up on the back of her neck.

Suddenly she noticed something white fluttering up in the balcony. Before Nancy could say anything, a high-pitched moan filled the room, and the white shape floated into a shaft of moonlight.

Then, as another moan filled the air, the ghostly form jumped off the balcony toward Nancy and her friends!

Chapter

Ten

I TOLD YOU there was a ghost!" Bess cried. "Let's get out of here!"

Nancy jumped to her feet and ran toward the white form, which fluttered just above the floor a few feet away from the circle of sleeping bags.

"What *is* that thing?" Ned said, behind her.

The white shape lightly touched the floor and flattened out, then went still. Nancy laughed when she realized what it was.

"It's a plain bedsheet, you guys!" she called out. Lifting the sheet, she found some hangers bent in the rough outline of a head and torso. "Someone must have thrown it from the balcony."

"How'd they get up there?" Andrew asked as

he and Bess joined Nancy and Ned by the sheet. "We didn't hear anybody come in."

Nancy was instantly alert, listening. "You guys, the person might still be there," she whispered excitedly, hurrying toward the back door to the dining room. "Wait here. I'm going to check the back door and balcony before the person has a chance to get away."

As Nancy ran down the back hall, she felt another rush of cold air. When she reached the door, it was open. She stuck her head outside and looked at the moonlit lake and at the path running behind the inn, but saw no sign of anyone.

Quickly she closed and bolted the door, then rushed back down the hallway to the ballroom.

"Well?" Ned asked.

Nancy shook her head in frustration. "Whoever it was probably got out the back door."

"Let's check out the rest of the inn, just in case the person's still hiding," Andrew suggested.

Turning on all the lights, Nancy, Ned, Bess, and Andrew scoured the inn, checking all the upstairs rooms, the lobby, the dining room, the kitchen, the library, and the basement. Up in the balcony the stereo was still warm, and the two cassette decks were empty and had been left open. Otherwise, they found no sign of anyone.

One good thing came out of the prank, though, Nancy reflected. Andrew now seemed less guilty than he had before. There was no way he could have rigged the ghost and the sound of shuffling feet himself while he was downstairs sitting on his sleeping bag. It was still possible that Andrew was working with someone, but Nancy doubted his partner was either of her top suspects—Julie or Master Blaster. They both had more reason to hurt him than help him.

"I can't believe the person got away again," Andrew said, frowning, as they all regathered in the ballroom after their search.

Ned gave Andrew a sympathetic smile and said, "At least we stopped him from doing any harm."

"Yeah," Bess agreed, sinking down on her sleeping bag. "I don't know about the rest of you happy campers, but I've had enough excitement. I'm ready to go to sleep."

"We might as well all call it a night," Nancy said. "I think we've seen all the special effects we're going to see. Besides, I want to get up bright and early and go to Bentley High School. It's time to check out that Bentley High Boneheads T-shirt."

"There it is," Ned said early Thursday morning as he and Nancy drove to Bentley, armed with directions from Andrew.

Bentley High School had just appeared over the top of the hill. It was a square, three-story granite building with a tall clock tower.

"I guess school's already in session," Nancy

said as she found a spot in the nearly full parking lot.

"That's what I like about college," Ned said. "We get longer holiday vacations."

They went in the main entrance and found themselves at one end of a long linoleum-floored corridor. Students were gathered by the bright orange lockers lining the walls along either side. After asking some students for directions to the administrative offices, Nancy and Ned went to the end of the long hall and turned right.

"Here we go," Nancy said, seeing an office marked Student Affairs.

Stepping inside, they found themselves in a large room with several tables and chairs and bookshelves lining the wall. The only desk was occupied by a pudgy woman with shoulder-length brown hair and glasses.

"Yearbooks," Ned said, nodding toward a bookshelf filled with identical purple and white books, each marked with a different year.

"May I help you?" the woman asked, looking sternly at Ned.

"Uh, yes," Nancy said. Thinking fast, she pulled her notepad and a pen from her purse and said, "We're reporters, and we're doing a piece called 'Whatever Happened to the Class of Seventy-seven.' It's a series of profiles of the graduates of Bentley High School. We were wondering if we could look at a few yearbooks, just as background."

Nancy held her breath, hoping the woman wouldn't ask what paper they worked for. To her relief, the woman simply shrugged and said, "Make sure to put them back when you're done."

With a wink at Ned Nancy walked over to the bookshelf and found the yearbook labeled 1977. Then she sat down at the table farthest from the woman and flipped it open to the table of contents. Ned pulled a chair up next to her.

"Seniors ... teachers ... sports ... clubs ... " she read, running her finger down the page.

"Try clubs," Ned suggested. "The Boneheads could be some special kind of organization."

Nancy flipped through the pages of black and white portraits, sports teams, and candid shots until she came to the club section.

"There it is!" Ned exclaimed in a hoarse whisper, jabbing a finger at a group photograph.

Nancy's heart jumped as she, too, spotted the Bentley High Boneheads logo. The word *Boneheads* was hand drawn, and each letter was shaped out of white bones, just as it had been on the T-shirt.

"What kind of club was it?" Ned asked softly, looking at the short paragraph under the logo.

Nancy read the paragraph aloud. " 'The Bentley Boneheads are proud of the contribution we've made to our school. We kept our grades low to balance the grade curve. We cut classes so our teachers would have more time for the other students, and we've spent lots of time in the vice principal's office so he wouldn't feel lonely. Party hearty!' "

Breaking into a deep laugh, Ned said, "I guess it wasn't a real club."

The woman at the desk gave them a questioning look, so Nancy punched Ned's arm. "Shh!" Then, turning her attention to the picture, she whispered, "It seems more like a spoof, or a bunch of friends clowning around."

Both the boys and the girls in the photograph had long hair, and most of them wore rock band T-shirts. All in all, there were about a dozen teenagers in two rows, making faces at the camera.

"There are names under the picture," Nancy said, squinting to read the tiny print. "Guy Lewis," she said excitedly, pointing at the third guy from the left in the back row. He was thin, with stringy dark hair and a goatee. "He's the only one with the initials G.L. It has to be him!"

Ned studied the photograph. "I still don't see what his connection to Andrew might be," he commented. "Andrew is years younger than this guy, and they're from different towns."

"Hmm," Nancy said. "It's probably just chance that Guy stayed overnight at the inn, but I'll call Chief McGinnis at the River Heights police station when we get back to the inn. Maybe he has something on this guy."

"Look at that girl Guy Lewis has his arm around," Ned commented, still looking at the photograph. "She looks like somebody, only I can't put my finger on who it is."

The girl was pretty, with hair pulled back into a sleek ponytail. She was slim and wore snugly fitting jeans and cowboy boots. "You're right, she does look familiar."

Once again Nancy scanned the names beneath the picture. When she read the one after Guy Lewis, she nearly fell out of her seat. But another look at the picture confirmed it. "Ned, we know that woman. We've been seeing her every day since Monday," Nancy said.

"Colleen O'Herlihy?" Ned said, reading the name. Then his dark eyes met Nancy's, and his mouth fell open. "You don't mean . . . ?"

Nancy nodded. "The Colleen in the photograph is actually Colleen Morgan!"

Chapter

Eleven

"YOU'RE RIGHT!" Ned exclaimed in a low voice. "It *is* her."

Her pulse racing, Nancy flipped forward in the yearbook to look for the graduation portraits of Guy and Colleen. There was no listing for Colleen O'Herlihy. Guy Lewis, though, was among the seniors. He wore a T-shirt instead of a shirt and tie, and nothing was listed under his picture except his name.

"Maybe Colleen graduated a different year," Ned suggested. He stood up to take out a few more yearbooks but had trouble getting them off the shelf because of his cast.

Nancy jumped up to help him. "Let's split

these up," she suggested. "I'll take seventy-three through seventy-six. You take seventy-eight through eighty-one."

They checked each yearbook thoroughly, but neither of them was able to find any record of Colleen O'Herlihy.

"I don't get it," Nancy said, her brows knitting together. "We know she went to school here. So why isn't she listed with any of the senior classes?"

"Maybe she never graduated," Ned suggested. "Or maybe she transferred to another school."

"That's a good possibility," Nancy said, nodding. "Especially since Colleen said she went to a private school. Maybe she transferred to a private school before graduation."

As Nancy and Ned stood up and began putting away the yearbooks, Ned said, "I wonder if Colleen knew Guy was hanging around the inn."

Nancy thought for a moment. "She didn't act as if she recognized any of the stuff we found in the basement," she said, "though she did seem very eager to clean it out. Maybe she didn't want us to figure out who the homeless person was or that she knew him."

"But what's the connection?" Ned asked. "Why would it matter if Colleen knew him?"

"Good question," Nancy said. "After I talk to Chief McGinnis, I hope I'll be able to answer it."

After thanking the woman at the desk, Nancy and Ned left Bentley High School and got back in

Nancy's Mustang. As Nancy pulled out of the parking lot and started back toward Moon Lake, Ned said, "So you're adding Colleen to your list of suspects?"

"Definitely," Nancy told him. "Not that her knowing Guy Lewis is a crime. For all we know, Guy Lewis just slept at the inn for a few days and moved on. But Colleen sure gave us a false impression of her upbringing. She made it seem as if she has always been rich and privileged, when it looks as if she was just a normal kid who went to public school."

"That's not a crime, either," Ned pointed out.

"If it were, we'd *all* be guilty," Nancy joked. "But my point is that if she hid that, there may be other things she's not telling us."

Ned nodded thoughtfully. "If Guy Lewis is still hanging around the inn, causing trouble, maybe Colleen knows he's there."

"She might not want anybody to know that she's helping him," Nancy added. "After all, she *is* married now. Her husband might not be too understanding if she was spending time with her old boyfriend."

When Nancy pulled into the Lakeside Inn parking lot a short while later, the red TeenWorks bus was already there, as well as some other cars and vans. She and Ned were about to get out of the parked Mustang when Master Blaster came out the inn's front door, wearing a faded denim jacket covered all over with buttons naming famous rock groups. He headed toward a beat-up blue hatchback parked near Nancy and Ned.

"Wait a minute," Nancy said, putting her hand on Ned's arm. "Let's see what he does."

The deejay opened the hatchback, and Nancy could see that it was loaded with shoe boxes. He rummaged in several of the boxes, pulling out half a dozen cassette tapes.

"So that's where he gets his music," Ned said.

At Ned's words a light suddenly blinked on in Nancy's mind. "Why didn't I think of it before?" she exclaimed softly, tapping her forehead with her palm. "Blaster said he uses sound effects when he does his original music. Maybe the ghost noises we heard came from his tapes."

Master Blaster slammed the hatchback shut, but the back door popped open again. After two more tries he finally managed to close it, then headed for the front entrance to the inn.

"Now's our chance," Nancy said as soon as Blaster disappeared inside. She hopped out of the Mustang and hurried over to the hatchback.

"Wow!" Ned exclaimed, coming up next to her and staring through the tinted glass. "Look at all those tapes."

The backseat of the car had been pushed down, leaving a large flat surface that was completely covered by shoe boxes filled with audiocassettes. Nancy estimated that there were at least five hundred tapes.

"It's hard to read the cases through the glass,"

she said, squinting. As she laid her hand against the glass for a closer look, the hatchback popped open a few inches.

Nancy and Ned exchanged a guilty glance. "It's already open," Ned said. "What's a few more inches?"

After opening the hatchback, they took a closer look inside. Most of the tapes were commercial recordings by popular artists, but there were two shoe boxes filled with cassette cases that had been neatly labeled by hand.

Nancy read the titles aloud. "'The Master's Super Mix Part Two' . . . 'High Voltage Party Tape' . . . 'Babies Crying.'"

"'Babies Crying'?" Ned echoed. "What kind of party tape is that?"

"It's not," Nancy replied, growing excited. She peered at the other tapes in the box. "Listen to these. 'Things Breaking'; 'Sneezes and Coughs'; 'Footsteps.'"

"Sound effects!" Ned exclaimed. "Here's 'Thunderstorms' and—"

Nancy didn't hear the rest of what Ned was saying because she'd just found what she was looking for. Right after "Footsteps" was a cassette labeled "Haunted House."

"I think we've hit the jackpot," she said softly, pulling out the cassette and showing it to Ned. "I'll bet you anything this is what we heard inside the inn."

"I *knew* it was Blaster!" Ned said triumphantly. "I just wish I'd brought my tape player so we could listen to it right here."

"We still can," Nancy told him, "on the cassette player in my car."

She quickly slipped the cassettes into the pocket of her parka, while Ned lowered the hatchback roof with his good hand.

After hurrying to the Mustang, Nancy got in behind the steering wheel, and Ned got in beside her. She reached into her jacket pocket and flipped open the "Haunted House" cassette case. Then she turned on the ignition and loaded the cassette into her tape player.

"Hey! What do you think you're doing?" an angry voice growled right outside her window.

Nancy jumped in her seat, then whirled around to see who was talking.

It was Master Blaster. His face was pressed close to Nancy's window, and he was glaring at her with cold, dark eyes.

Chapter

Twelve

A CHILL RAN THROUGH Nancy's entire body as Blaster's furious gaze bored into her.

"Give me back my tape!" Blaster went on angrily. "I saw you steal it."

Nancy unrolled her window slowly, trying to think of what to say. "We didn't steal it," she told him. "We borrowed it."

"We were planning to put it right back," Ned added.

"Yeah, sure," Blaster said, glowering. "You were probably going to make copies of my dance mixes and sell them to some local deejay."

Was he honestly worried about his dance mix? Nancy wondered, trying to read the look in his eyes. Or was that just a cover for what he was really afraid of—that Nancy had caught the person who was trying to scare Andrew off the renovation.

"Actually," Nancy said evenly, "I'm not interested in your dance mixes. I'm more curious about your sound effects."

"Same difference," Blaster said. "I spent a lot of time putting those together. I don't want anybody else to get their hands on them."

Nancy took the "Haunted House" tape out of the player and showed it to Blaster. "We know that someone is trying to scare us away from the place, and twice now we've heard ghostly noises inside the inn," she said. "If these tapes match the sounds we've heard, you're going to look guilty. If they don't, it will help clear you."

"I don't need to be cleared!" Blaster shouted. "I didn't do anything wrong!"

"Then prove it," Ned challenged him. "Let us listen to the tape."

Master Blaster stuffed his hands into the pockets of his jacket. "Fine," he said hotly. "I've got nothing to hide. Go ahead and play it."

Nancy once more loaded the "Haunted House" tape into her player. Her heart started to beat faster as she pressed the Play button.

"*Aaaaaaaaaaagh!*" The tormented cry filled Nancy's car, giving Nancy a creepy feeling. The wails sounded just like the ones they'd all heard the first day at the inn.

"Sound familiar, Ned?" Nancy asked.

"Very," he replied, nodding.

Master Blaster's face turned bright red. "You don't know what you're talking about," he said.

Nancy pressed the Stop button and faced the deejay squarely. "Where were you last night, around ten o'clock?" she asked.

"What difference does it make?" Blaster demanded.

"Because that's when we heard some of these sound effects," she answered. "Right before a white sheet came flying off the balcony in the ballroom, rigged to look like a ghost."

Blaster looked from Nancy to Ned, then started to laugh. "Give me a break," he scoffed. "Who'd pull a stupid trick like that?"

"Don't pretend you don't remember," Ned said. "You must have set it up yourself, right after you turned on the stereo."

The deejay held up his hands defensively. "Look, man, I wasn't anywhere near the inn last night!"

"That's funny, because your tapes were," Nancy shot back.

"Well, someone must have borrowed them, like you just tried to," Blaster contended. "They could have made copies and put the originals back when I wasn't looking."

He was putting on a good show of innocence, Nancy had to admit. But that didn't change the fact that he'd acted suspiciously after some of the accidents. Pressing the Eject button, she put the tape in its box and gave it to Blaster.

"Why are you so determined to blame me for something I didn't do?" Blaster demanded, taking the cassette. "I know you've been talking to my grandmother. Well, I'm warning you now. Stay away from her!"

Ned leaned across Nancy to say, "What are you so afraid of, Blaster? That we'll find out the truth about you? Like the fact that you used to go out with Julie Ross?"

Blaster hesitated, then said angrily, "My personal life is none of your business."

"It is when it could explain all the trouble going on here," Nancy said. "Maybe you're jealous of Andrew because he took Julie away from you. Sabotaging his renovation project would be a good way of getting back at him."

Blaster gaped at her. "Why would I want to do that?" he demanded. "Andrew promised me I can be the deejay at the dance club here when the inn opens. It's not big time or anything, but it would be a good start for my career."

Nancy fell silent. He had a good point, and she doubted he was lying—he had to know she could easily check his story with Andrew. Still, that didn't let him off the hook completely.

Giving Master Blaster a hard look, Nancy asked, "Then what were you doing by the back door Monday afternoon, right after we heard the ghost noises? And don't tell me you were just getting some air."

Blaster drew in a deep breath and let it out slowly. After a long silence he admitted, "I was trying to decide what to do about the fact that I'd just seen my ex-girlfriend running away from the inn. Yes, I saw Julie. I saw her the second time, too, right after Ned fell."

Nancy nodded. That explained the clay on the light switch and the wall.

"If you saw her, why didn't you say anything?" Ned asked.

"Even if she's the one causing the trouble, I didn't want to turn her in," Blaster answered with a guilty look. "I still care about her, even after everything she did to me. Oh, why am I even bothering to explain anything to you? I can see you don't believe me."

With a disgusted look at Nancy and Ned, Blaster turned and stalked back to the inn.

"You don't really believe him, do you, Nan?" Ned asked when Blaster had disappeared inside.

"I don't know," Nancy said. "I think he's telling the truth about having seen Julie. That would explain why he was so nervous when I asked him what he saw the day he was up in the alcove."

As she and Ned got out of the Mustang, Ned said, "I guess things don't look good for Julie now, do they?"

Nancy shook her head. "I still want to check

out Guy Lewis and his connection to Colleen Morgan, too," she said. "Come on. Let's go find Andrew. I want to use his phone to call Chief McGinnis."

When they got inside the inn, they didn't see Andrew, or anyone else for that matter, on the first floor. Finally Nancy and Ned found Andrew, Bess, Colleen, and what looked like the entire TeenWorks crew in the basement.

At first it looked as if there was more junk piled up in the basement than there'd been the day before. Then Nancy noticed that only the area near the bottom of the stairs was crowded with old furniture and newspapers. The rest of the basement was nearly empty.

"We've got a good system going," Andrew explained, spotting Nancy and Ned. "It's like a bucket brigade. Once we get everything near the stairs, we're going to pass it up hand to hand. We ought to be finished by the time the haulers get here after lunch. Then we'll be on schedule to pour the concrete floor in the morning."

Nancy was relieved to see that Andrew still seemed dedicated to keeping the renovation going. Maybe she'd been wrong to think he was sabotaging the inn to get the insurance money.

"Listen, I'll come down and help you move stuff in a few minutes," she told Andrew. "Meanwhile, could I use the phone in your office, Andrew? I've got to make a quick call."

"Sure," Andrew said.

Nancy hurried back up the stairs to the lobby, entered Andrew's office, and closed the door behind her. Seconds later she was dialing the number of the River Heights police headquarters.

"Hello, Nancy," Chief McGinnis greeted her warmly when the call was put through to him. "Don't tell me you're on another case."

"It must be fate," Nancy joked. "But listen, I was wondering if you could check somebody out for me. His name's Guy Lewis. He graduated from Bentley High School in 1977."

Nancy explained about the sabotage and pranks at the inn and told the chief about finding evidence that Lewis may have been there recently.

"I'll have to run a check and get back to you," Chief McGinnis told her.

"Could you also check out a woman named Colleen Morgan or Colleen O'Herlihy?" Nancy asked.

There was a long pause before the police chief inquired, "You mean the wife of Frederick Morgan, as in Morgan Lumber, Morgan Steel, Morgan Financial Services . . . ?"

"That's the one. It looks as if she went to high school with Lewis. Not that that necessarily means anything, but if there's any connection between them, I'd like to know what it is."

"I'll put someone on this right away," Chief McGinnis said. "Where do you want me to call you with the information?"

Nancy thought for a moment. "I'll call you," she decided. "Colleen Morgan's working here at the inn. I don't want to risk her overhearing me. Why don't I try you in an hour or two?"

"Good enough," the chief agreed. "We should have something by then."

After thanking him, Nancy hung up. When she returned to the basement, everyone was moving the last of the furniture to the base of the stairs.

Nancy wanted to ask Andrew whether he'd really offered Blaster the deejay job, but Blaster was right next to him, helping him move a dresser. Seeing Bess and Natalia Diaz struggling to carry a fire-blackened mattress from a pile of them at the back of the basement, Nancy went over to help. They dumped it near some others near the stairs, then returned to the back wall for another.

"Phew," Nancy said as she grabbed one end of the mattress. "This thing stinks."

Wrinkling up her nose, Bess added, "From the smell down here, you'd think the fire happened yesterday instead of fifty years ago."

"My eyes are watering," Natalia put in. "The first thing Andrew should do once we clear out this stuff is fumigate the place."

Nancy's eyes were beginning to water, too, and her throat felt dry. There was a choking, bitter smell in the air.

Suddenly she paused and cocked her head.

"Do you smell something?" Nancy asked Bess and Natalia.

Natalia nodded. "It's getting hard to breathe. And it's getting hot in here, too."

"It's the exercise," Bess said, grunting under the weight of the mattress. "All this heavy lifting is making us burn calories faster—"

"I don't think so," Nancy interrupted. She dropped her corner of the mattress, a feeling of dread welling up in the pit of her stomach. A moment later she pointed in horror at the huge pile of broken wooden furniture directly between them and the stairwell.

A thick plume of choking, black smoke rose from the pile, rapidly filling the basement. Already the other teens in the basement were coughing and rubbing their eyes.

As Nancy watched, the huge pile of furniture erupted into flames. Almost instantly everything was awash in a searing orange blaze.

"Let's get out of here!" Nancy cried.

She pulled Bess and Natalia toward the stairs, but their way was blocked by a wall of rapidly spreading flames. The other teens were scrambling around the burning debris, too, looking for an escape route.

Within seconds the fire had completely engulfed the base of the stairs, and Nancy realized the awful truth.

They were trapped in an underground inferno, and there was no way out!

Chapter

Thirteen

W E'RE GOING TO DIE!" Bess cried. The other teenagers started screaming, too.

Nancy's eyes and lungs were burning, but she tried to remain calm. "Stay low, everybody!" she yelled. "And keep your nose and mouth covered!"

As the others obeyed, Nancy squinted through the heavy smoke. If she didn't find some way out, they'd all be fried to a crisp in minutes.

"I never should have piled all that stuff in front of the stairs!" Andrew yelled from close by. His black hair was plastered to his sweat-soaked forehead, and his round glasses reflected twin orange flames. "What an idiot I was!"

Coughing, Nancy searched desperately for an

escape route. The flames extended all the way around the stairs, but she saw that some parts of the fire burned higher than others. The flames rising from the damp, moldy mattresses were only a foot or so high.

"That's it!" Nancy exclaimed, picking up the mattress she, Bess, and Natalia Diaz had dropped. "We'll make a pathway."

"What are you talking about?" Bess asked.

"We've still got a bunch of mattresses we haven't moved yet," Nancy told her, pointing to the ones piled against the stone wall. "We can drop them over the burning mattresses. That should smother the flames long enough for us to get out of here."

"Good idea," Ned said, then broke into a cough as smoke filled his lungs. "Everybody, grab a mattress!"

Nancy, Bess, and Natalia dumped their mattress on a smoldering pile near the stairs. Then some of the other teens laid their mattresses upright on either side, making a temporary protective wall. When two more mattresses were down, they formed a path to the stairs.

"Now run!" Nancy cried out, urging the others over the lumpy, hot mattresses. When everyone had gone ahead, she and Andrew brought up the rear. Just as she made it to the bottom step, the pile of mattresses burst into flame.

Nancy nearly scorched her hand as it came to rest for a split second against the metal banister.

Jerking it away, she scrambled up the stairs and staggered into the lobby.

Gasping for breath, she ran for Andrew's office so she could call the fire department. Before she even got to Andrew's door, however, she heard the wail of approaching sirens outside.

Was the fire department really on its way already? Nancy wondered, pausing. How could that be? The fire had started just a few minutes ago, and everyone at the inn had been stuck in the basement. Who had alerted the fire fighters?

Joining the sweaty, red-faced crowd rushing for the front door, Nancy saw two bright red fire trucks just pulling up the curved driveway.

"I don't believe it!" Andrew cried, standing on the front doorstep of the inn. "How did they know?"

"That's what I was wondering," Nancy said as the fire trucks screeched to a halt and a dozen fire fighters in black raincoats, helmets, and rubber boots jumped out.

"It's in the basement," Andrew directed them as they rushed inside. "Follow me." After instructing the TeenWorks crew to remain outside, he followed the fire fighters inside.

For a few minutes Nancy wandered through the crowd, looking for Ned and Bess. But before she found her friends, Nancy spotted a familiar mass of brown curls with a copper streak.

Julie Ross was rushing through the chaos of fire fighters and distraught teenagers. Tears were streaming down her grief-stricken face. "Andrew!" she called, her voice breaking. "Where are you?"

It seemed obvious that Julie still cared about Andrew. She must have come running from the boutique the second she heard the sirens. But then Nancy remembered Julie's angry words the first time she'd spoken to her at the crafts store: "I hope that old dump burns to the ground."

Nancy frowned, wondering if it could be mere coincidence that Julie was so close to the inn just minutes after a fire started. Even if she'd been at her boutique nearby and had smelled smoke, she couldn't possibly have gotten to the inn so fast. Maybe Julie's display of concern for Andrew was just an act to cover up the fact that she was the one to start the fire.

Just as Nancy was about to follow Julie, someone grabbed her arm. She turned to see Ned standing there, a relieved look on his face.

"The fire's out," he told her.

"Already?" Nancy asked. She checked over her shoulder and saw that Julie was still milling in the crowd outside the inn. Nancy resolved to keep her within eyesight.

Ned nodded. "Fortunately for Andrew, it was contained in that one area and didn't spread," he told her. "The fire fighters were able to douse it pretty quickly."

More sirens echoed through the bare trees, and three Melborne Township police cars pulled up the driveway alongside the fire trucks. Half a dozen officers got out.

A tall female officer and her partner, a beefy red-haired man, got out of the car nearest the inn's entrance. "Andrew Lockwood?" the female officer called.

Andrew appeared in the front entrance of the inn, his sweatshirt sooty and his glasses fogged with smoke. "I'm Andrew Lockwood."

"I'm Lieutenant Oscarson. I'd like to ask you a few questions," the female officer said, taking out a leather-bound notepad. "Are you the owner of this place?"

Andrew walked down the steps and paused a few feet away from Lieutenant Oscarson. "My father is. I'm renovating it for him."

"Yet you've taken out an accident insurance policy on the inn in your name, with yourself as the beneficiary?" the lieutenant inquired.

Andrew took off his glasses and began wiping them nervously on his sweatshirt. "Uh . . . that was my father's idea," he said. "He wants to give me the inn after it's finished. I know how it must look. . . ."

Lieutenant Oscarson fixed Andrew with a stern glare. "About fifteen minutes ago we got an anonymous tip telling us there was a fire at the inn and that the fire was arson," she told him. "We were also told that you'd recently increased your insurance policy. That makes you our prime suspect."

Andrew's eyes grew wide with panic. "That's not true!" he protested. "I mean, I did increase my coverage, but I *didn't* start this fire."

"I can vouch for him," Ned said, looking straight at the police officer. "I was with him every second before the fire started. He didn't do anything except move some old furniture around."

There was something else about the officer's accusation that struck Nancy as odd, too. Stepping forward, she told Lieutenant Oscarson, "There *was* no fire fifteen minutes ago, when the call came. It started less than ten minutes ago, which was *after* you got the tip. Doesn't that seem odd?"

The lieutenant quickly flipped through her notepad. "We haven't yet determined the exact time the fire started."

"The call had to come before the fire started," Nancy insisted. "None of us had a chance to call the fire department after we got out of the basement, yet the fire trucks were here as soon as we got upstairs. I think the person who called is the arsonist. How else could he or she have known in advance that a fire would happen?"

"In that case it doesn't make sense that Andrew would do it," Ned put in. "If he wanted to torch the inn and collect on the insurance, I doubt he would have called the fire department and the police department and given himself away."

Lieutenant Oscarson leaned back against the hood of her police car and studied Nancy and Ned carefully. "You're saying the caller named Andrew to take suspicion off himself?"

"Or herself," Nancy amended. "Do you have any idea who called in the tip? Even knowing whether it was a man or a woman could be helpful."

Making a note in her pad, the officer said, "One of our emergency operators took the call. I'll try to track it down. Meanwhile, I've still got to take Andrew down to the station for questioning." She stood up and opened the back door to her car.

"See you guys later," Andrew said glumly, getting into the backseat.

Ned's brown eyes flashed angrily as he watched the police car roll down the driveway. "I know he didn't do it," he insisted. "We have to do something."

"I'm going to start by calling Chief McGinnis," Nancy assured him, "to see what he turned up on Colleen and Guy Lewis."

Dodging the fire fighters who were leaving the building with their hoses and hatchets, Nancy hurried to Andrew's office.

"Appears we've got something on Lewis," Chief McGinnis said over the line a few moments later.

Nancy's heart started beating faster. "He's got a record?"

The chief whistled. "I'll say he does. He's been convicted of burglary, vagrancy, extortion, and about fifteen years back he belonged to a theft ring that stole audio equipment from warehouses and sold it illegally."

"Wow," Nancy said. "I can see why Colleen wouldn't want anybody to know she knew him. He sounds like bad news."

"It also says here that Lewis was just released from the state prison a few weeks ago," McGinnis added.

Nancy thought quickly. "That could explain what he was doing in the basement," she said. "It looked as if he was here fairly recently. Maybe he thought this place was still abandoned, so he came here to stay when he got out of jail. Unless he had some other purpose. I wonder if there's any link between Lewis and the Lockwood family?"

"Could be," came the chief's voice over the line. "I know some of the guys in the Melborne Police Department. I'll see if they can help out on this."

"Thanks," Nancy told him. "There's something else I don't understand," she went on. "Where's Guy Lewis now? From what I can tell, he's not at the inn anymore. But I think he may be behind what's happened here. Or maybe he's working with Colleen Morgan. Did you find anything on her?"

"Not a thing," Chief McGinnis told Nancy.

"I looked up O'Herlihy and Morgan. She's clean."

Thanking him again, Nancy hung up. She exited through the inn's front entrance just as two officers were sealing the door with yellow tape marked Police Line—Do Not Cross.

Outside, the last of the fire fighters were getting on their trucks and pulling out of the driveway. Nancy spotted Ned and Bess nearby, standing at the edge of the parking lot. The other teens also milled around, as if they weren't sure whether to go back to work or go home.

"I told Bess what we found out about Colleen at Bentley High," Ned said when Nancy joined them. "Did the police find anything on Colleen?"

Nancy shook her head. "Her old friend Guy Lewis has a record, though. And we're not just talking parking tickets."

"Could they have been working together?" Bess wondered. "Colleen could have set the fire, and Lewis could have placed the call."

"It's possible," Nancy agreed.

"What about Blaster?" Ned wanted to know. "He could have set the fire."

Bess started to object, but Nancy said, "He's right, Bess. Blaster was down in the basement with us, but he could have sneaked away at some point to place the call. We were too busy to watch everyone the whole time."

"Julie could have done it, too," Bess argued. "I know I saw her wandering around just now, calling Andrew's name. She's got curly hair with a red streak in it, right?"

Nancy nodded, remembering that she still hadn't had a chance to question Julie. Nancy searched the crowd with her eyes, but Julie had disappeared.

"That's the third time Julie's been at the inn with no explanation," Nancy said. "But she wasn't in the basement when the fire started."

"Do you think she could have sneaked down the stairs and started the fire while we all were working?" Ned asked.

"I doubt she could have done it without someone spotting her," Nancy said.

A loud voice broke into their conversation. "Attention!" shouted a police officer. He stood on the doorstep, holding a megaphone to his mouth. "This area is now off-limits. Please go home and wait for further instructions."

There was a collective groan from the TeenWorks teenagers, who were gathered around Colleen.

"Hey, Ms. Morgan," Blaster said. "Does that mean the party's canceled for tonight?"

"Of course not," Colleen answered at once. "With all the bad things that have happened, we need a party now more than ever. Everybody be at my place at eight o'clock sharp, or else!"

Chapter

Fourteen

A<small>S THE TEENAGERS CHEERED</small>, Bess grinned at Nancy and Ned. "I'm glad Colleen has her priorities straight. We could use a party around here."

"Mmm," Nancy murmured distractedly. Seeing that Colleen was about to leave, she hurried over to her, hoping to question her about her relationship with Guy Lewis. "Colleen, could I talk to you a minute?" Nancy asked.

"Sorry," Colleen told her. "I don't have time right now."

"But it's important," Nancy insisted. "I'm trying to locate a man named Guy Lewis. I think he might be responsible for what's going on here."

Colleen's freckled face was blank. "Who?"

"His name is Guy Lewis. I think he's the person who was sleeping in the basement."

Shrugging, Colleen said, "The name doesn't sound familiar. Why are you asking me?"

Nancy's blue eyes bored into Colleen. It seemed unlikely that she wouldn't have the slightest recollection of a guy she'd known in high school. Colleen was definitely hiding something. But whether it was simply the fact that she knew Lewis, or something more, remained to be seen.

"I thought you might remember him from high school," Nancy prodded. *"Bentley* High School . . ."

Nancy saw a flicker of unease in Colleen's green eyes. Colleen glanced quickly at her gold watch, then said, "I'd love to talk to you, but I've got to bring these kids back to the TeenWorks center, and then I have to rush home and prepare for the party. We'll talk tonight, okay?"

Turning away from Nancy, Colleen called out to the TeenWorks kids and started down the driveway to the parking lot. Nancy let out a sigh of frustration as she watched the other woman.

Colleen is definitely hiding something, Nancy thought. And tonight, at the party, I'm going to try to find out exactly what it is.

"This house is incredible," Bess said to Nancy and Ned a few hours later as they entered Colleen

Morgan's mansion. The foyer had polished wooden floors and an enormous crystal chandelier hanging overhead. Intricately patterned Persian rugs were scattered over the floor, and a grand staircase swept upward to the second floor.

After a butler had taken their coats and jackets, a maid led the three teens down a long hallway with oil paintings hanging along the walls and more Persian rugs.

"This is my kind of house," Bess said approvingly.

The thumping bass line of a rock song grew louder as they neared a pair of carved wooden doors at the end of the hall. The maid ushered them through the doors, and Nancy found herself in a living room almost as large as the ballroom at the inn. Groupings of sofas and velvet chairs were spaced around the room, and the walls were paneled with deep red-brown mahogany.

Along one wall several tables were set up, covered with white linen and loaded with food. Uniformed caterers stood behind the tables, serving cold cuts, fruit, and hot dishes in silver warming trays. A makeshift sound system had been set up at the far end of the room and was connected to two six-foot-high speakers.

"Not bad for something Colleen just threw together in a day," Nancy joked, watching the TeenWorks kids, as well as the construction foreman and the master electrician, dancing in a cleared space in the middle of the room.

"I wonder where Andrew is," Ned said, looking around. "Do you think the police would keep him at the station this long?"

"It's hard to say," Nancy told him. "He's had a long day. Maybe he just didn't feel like going to a party."

Nancy turned as Colleen broke through the crowd and came toward them. She wore a royal blue minidress covered entirely in sequins. Her red hair was swept up in a French twist, and she wore diamond and sapphire earrings with a matching necklace. Her hand was nestled in the arm of a distinguished-looking man with graying hair and warm, intelligent eyes.

"Wow!" Bess whispered to Nancy. "I wonder how much that outfit cost."

Looking down at her own purple sweater dress, Nancy said, "I feel like a slob next to her." The dressiest thing she had on was the heart-shaped pendant Ned had given her the year before for Valentine's Day.

"Hi, guys," Colleen greeted them. "I'd like you to meet my husband, Frederick Morgan."

Nancy, Ned, and Bess all shook the hand he offered. "Nice to meet you, Mr. Morgan," Nancy said.

"Please call me Fred," Colleen's husband told them. "And please, start eating right away. I think we ordered way too much food."

"I'll do my best," Bess said cheerfully, heading straight for the catering tables.

"I'm sure you'll find everything you'd like," Frederick Morgan assured Nancy and Ned. "When my wife plans a party, she thinks of everything." He wrapped an arm around Colleen's waist and pulled her close, planting an affectionate kiss on her cheek. "I don't know what I'd do without her."

Colleen looked lovingly into her husband's eyes and stroked the graying hair above his temples. "I don't even want to *think* of what I'd do without you."

"Let's mingle," Ned murmured in Nancy's ear. "I feel like I'm intruding."

With a smile Nancy grabbed Ned's hand and they left the Morgans. Then her smile vanished. "It still doesn't make sense to me," she said in a low voice. "Colleen seems to have everything—looks, money, a wonderful husband . . ."

"Yeah," Ned agreed. "It sort of rules her out as a suspect, doesn't it? I mean, why would she want to make trouble at the inn when her life is going so well?"

"That's the part that doesn't make sense," Nancy said. "If she hasn't done anything wrong, then what's she acting so secretive about? I'm going to try to talk to her one more time."

Nancy waited until she saw Colleen alone, clearing some empty glasses off a coffee table, then strode purposefully toward her. As soon as Colleen spotted her coming, however, she skirted away through the crowd. Before Nancy could reach her, Colleen rejoined her husband, and the two of them wandered out a side door.

"She's avoiding me, I'm sure of it," Nancy said, reappearing at Ned's side. She paused as Blaster's voice boomed out over a microphone.

"Listen up, partiers, it's the music meister," Blaster said. He stood next to the makeshift sound system, wearing a baggy red shirt over faded blue jeans. "You've heard Top Forty tonight, but now it's time for a blast from Master B. You can tell your grandchildren you heard the tune here first—'Bust 'Em Up' by the soon-to-be-famous recording star Master Blaster. I do it louder and faster!

"Yay!" Bess cheered. She was standing just a few feet away from Blaster, looking on encouragingly as he slipped a tape into the stereo and turned it on. First Nancy heard the sounds of cars crashing and glass breaking, followed by a driving beat and catchy riff of synthesized music.

"Not bad," Ned said, tapping his feet.

Nancy automatically started bobbing her head to the beat. "He's talented," she agreed. "But I'm more worried about Bess than the quality of the music." She frowned as Blaster grabbed Bess's hands and led her into a small group of people who were already dancing.

"I'll keep an eye on him," Ned promised.

"You're the best, Nickerson," Nancy said, grinning.

Ned tapped her nose. "It's about time you

noticed," he said warmly. "Uh-oh, you have that look on your face," he added. "What are you planning, Nan?"

"I'm going to look around the house a bit and see if I can learn more about Colleen."

Ned gave her a kiss on the cheek and said, "Good luck. I'll be right here if you need me."

Nancy slipped out the door and followed the hallway back to the foyer. After seeing that none of the servants were around, she raced up the stairs, where she found another hallway. There were so many doors on either side of it that Nancy didn't know where to begin.

She moved quickly and silently, opening the doors one by one. After seeing a workout room with weight-lifting equipment and several bedrooms that didn't look lived in, Nancy opened the door to a room that was larger than the others. It held two dressers, an armchair, and a canopied bed with an embroidered white spread and a dozen white lace pillows. A pair of jeans and a silk blouse lay discarded on the bed.

Jackpot! thought Nancy. This had to be Colleen and Fred's room.

After entering quietly, Nancy closed the door behind her and started opening some of the dresser drawers. All she found were clothes, lingerie, scarves, jewelry, and other accessories. So far it looked as if the only thing Colleen was guilty of was having a fabulous wardrobe.

Then Nancy noticed an interior door, slightly

ajar. Padding softly over the plush white carpet, she opened the door and entered a smaller room with sleek, modern furniture. White shelves lined with books ran around all four walls, with a white laminated counter and drawers beneath. On the counter were a personal computer, laser printer, and fax machine.

Nancy checked over her shoulder to make sure she was still alone, then started going through the drawers beneath the counter. The top drawers held pencils, pens, office supplies, and stationery with Colleen's initials at the top. Lower down Nancy found old invitations from charity balls and several drawers full of photographs of Colleen and her husband.

As Nancy pulled out a deep bottom drawer, her pulse quickened. On top of a jumble of papers were a soldering iron, a drill, and several drill bits—the tools that had been taken from the inn.

Digging beneath the tools, Nancy saw that the drawer was loaded with old programs from school plays and ballet recitals, some dating twenty years back. At last, something from Colleen's past! Now Nancy could see if Colleen really had lied about her background.

Nancy gasped as she recognized a purple and white yearbook dated 1977. It was the same one she and Ned had seen that morning at Bentley High.

After carefully easing the yearbook out so that she wouldn't disturb anything else in the drawer,

Nancy started flipping to the pictures of graduating seniors. The yearbook fell open to the page with Guy Lewis's picture, and Nancy found a white envelope tucked inside.

"Hmm—" she said aloud, picking up the envelope. It was addressed to Colleen and had no return address, but the post office stamp was dated just a few weeks earlier.

Opening the envelope, Nancy saw that it contained several separate letters. And they were all from Guy Lewis!

Nancy skimmed the first one quickly:

Dear Colleen,

Remember old Guy? I bet you'd rather forget—ha-ha. I finally got out of prison after five long years. I need money real bad, and you're just the person to give it to me.

Why should you give old Guy a break? Because if you don't, I'll tell your rich husband that you were part of the theft ring back in high school. That won't sound too good when they write you up in the social register. I'll bet your husband might even divorce you when he finds out you've been keeping dirty secrets.

I'll only keep quiet if you give me fifty thousand dollars, time and place to be arranged. You'll be hearing from me soon.

Guy

Guy was trying to blackmail Colleen! Nancy felt light-headed as she quickly read the other letters.

Guy wrote that he had newspaper clippings detailing Colleen's arrest and the fact that she had served time in a juvenile detention center. He said he'd hidden the clippings in the basement of the Lakeside Inn when he'd passed through there. He also threatened to take them to Colleen's husband if she didn't come up with the money. There was no letter telling Colleen where to meet Guy and drop the money, but Nancy had seen enough.

No wonder Colleen had volunteered to work at the inn. She'd been trying to find the newspaper articles and destroy them before Guy used them to destroy her life.

That explained why she'd spent so much time in the basement with the old newspapers. She probably thought the articles about her were hidden among them. And she'd been trying to scare everyone else away from the inn because she'd been afraid someone else would find the articles before she did.

"What are you doing here?"

Nancy jumped and whirled around to find Colleen standing in the open doorway to the study. Colleen's green eyes flashed as she stared at the letters in Nancy's hand, and there was a tense set to her jaw. Nancy had been caught red-handed!

"Don't even bother trying to think of an excuse," Colleen went on. Her face became an icy mask as she snatched the letters from Nancy's hand, then reached toward a bottom drawer Nancy hadn't yet examined. "I know exactly what you're doing here. You're a real snoop, aren't you?"

Nancy rose slowly to her feet, letting the yearbook slide to the floor. Her eyes darted quickly around as she tried to find a way out of the room. There was a second door in the opposite wall, but Nancy wasn't sure where it led.

"Oh, yes," Colleen said, opening the drawer. "You're leaving, all right. But you're leaving with *me!*"

In one swift motion Colleen pulled a gun out of the drawer and aimed it right at Nancy!

Chapter

Fifteen

NANCY FORCED HERSELF to breathe deeply, fighting the fear that was welling inside her. She didn't want to make any sudden moves that might make Colleen react rashly.

"You're not really going to use that," Nancy said, trying to keep her voice firm.

"Try me," Colleen said, cocking the trigger of the gun.

"How are you going to explain a dead body to your husband?" Nancy prodded. "That's going to be a lot harder than telling him you did time for stealing."

A tiny muscle in Colleen's cheek twitched. "So you read about that, huh? Well, you're going to take that secret to your grave. I'll just tell Fred you were trying to steal my jewelry. I'll say the gun is yours and it went off accidentally. It's unregistered, so Fred will never know I was the one who pulled the trigger."

Nancy shivered at the cool, matter-of-fact way Colleen was talking about murder. So much for the selfless socialite who wanted to make the world a better place.

"You'd do anything to hide the truth from him, wouldn't you?" Nancy challenged.

"You bet I would," Colleen said. "He's the best thing that ever happened to me. Nobody's going to ruin what we have together." She frowned slightly. "But you have a point—a dead body will ruin the carpet. Turn around, slowly, and open the other door."

Stalling for time, Nancy asked, "Where are we going?"

"Never mind where. Just open the door and start walking."

Nancy's mind raced, trying to figure a way out. She had to obey Colleen, but at least she could leave something behind, some sign so her friends would know she'd been here.

Reaching up as if to scratch her neck, Nancy undid the clasp of the pendant Ned had given her for Valentine's Day and let the pendant slip down the front of her sweater to the white carpet. Then, opening the other door of the study, she entered a narrow, dimly lit back stairway. As she made her way down the stairs, she was acutely aware of the hard barrel of Colleen's gun pressed against her back.

"Now, down the hall and out the door," Colleen directed.

Nancy did as she was told and found herself in a four-car garage. The car nearest her was a dark green Jaguar. Colleen gestured for Nancy to get in behind the wheel, while Colleen got in beside her. The car keys were dangling from the ignition.

Pressing a small remote clipped to the sun visor, Colleen opened one of the garage doors. "Drive," she commanded.

"Where are we going?" Nancy asked.

"To the inn. We're going to put an end to this once and for all. You're going to disappear very mysteriously, without a trace, in fact. Even if they question me about it, they'll never be able to pin anything on me."

Nancy gripped the wheel tightly to keep her hands from trembling as she backed the car out of the garage and turned it around.

"You won't get away with this," she said firmly, turning onto the quiet street with its large, stately homes. "The police and my friends already know about your connection to Guy Lewis. If anything happens to me, they'll know you were responsible."

"The fact that I knew Guy in high school

means nothing," Colleen said. "No one else around here knows I was involved in anything illegal, and I don't have a record."

Nancy's curiosity got the better of her fear, and she asked, "Why don't the police know about your involvement with the theft ring?"

"I was only fifteen when I got arrested," Colleen said. "If you're convicted as a minor, they wipe your slate clean when you turn eighteen."

"How convenient for you," Nancy said dryly.

"It was, until Guy came back into my life," Colleen said. The gun in her hand glinted as they passed beneath the streetlights. "Now that you know about it, too, I'll have to take care of both of you."

Glancing at Colleen, Nancy said, "But other people must have known about it, since it was in the papers."

"That was years ago," Colleen said. "It only made the local papers, anyway. When I got out of juvenile hall, my parents moved to another town and put me in a private school where no one knew me. I got a fresh start. I did better in school, and I got into a good college. I turned my life around."

"And look where you are today," Nancy said. "You've moved up to murdering an innocent person."

Colleen shifted uncomfortably in her seat. "Today doesn't count. Once you're out of the picture, I'll go back to my wonderful life with

Fred. He's such a kind, generous man. I can't let him find out about my past. I'm afraid he really would divorce me. Then where would I be?"

Nancy couldn't believe how twisted Colleen was. She actually thought it was worse to lose a rich husband than to kill someone!

Soon Nancy turned onto the winding road leading up to Moon Lake. The road was pitch-black, with no streetlights, so she could only judge where she was going by the double yellow lines illuminated by her headlights.

"I didn't want to hurt anybody," Colleen said after a short silence. "I was just trying to scare people away until I could find the evidence and get rid of it. But everyone was down there in the basement with me, and there was so much stuff. There was no way I could find the articles quickly. I had to create a diversion to buy time."

"You call pushing Ned off the balcony a diversion?" Nancy asked angrily.

"I didn't have anything to do with that," Colleen insisted with a dismissive wave of her gun. "That must have been an accident."

Colleen actually sounded sincere, but considering the situation, Nancy wasn't about to give her the benefit of the doubt.

"What about the chandelier?" Nancy demanded. "I suppose that was an accident, too?"

Colleen's green eyes gleamed with satisfaction. "Nope. I severed the cable the night before, as you so cleverly deduced."

"And you made a copy of Andrew's keys?" Nancy guessed.

"Very good," Colleen complimented her. "Too bad I couldn't get one to the basement, or none of this might have happened. Andrew only has one copy of that key, and he keeps it in his pocket."

"I'll bet you stole Blaster's sound-effects tapes, too," Nancy said.

Colleen bristled. "I didn't steal them, I borrowed them. I put the keys back, and the tapes, too, after I'd made copies."

Nancy didn't bother to mention that Colleen hadn't returned the soldering iron and drill. "And that sheet you rigged up to look like a ghost—that was to scare Andrew off the renovation, wasn't it?"

"I heard Blaster mention ghost stories, so I figured the subject would eventually come up during your little sleepover," Colleen said. "Too bad Andrew didn't take the hint."

"And the dummy we found hanging in the noose?"

"Me again," Colleen said, almost proudly.

"And of course you're the one who wrote the threatening notes and called in the arson tip to the police," Nancy said. "But if you were trying to frame Andrew, it didn't work. I spoke to the officer at the scene and told her the call came *before* the fire."

"So what?" Colleen asked as Nancy pulled into the empty parking lot of the Lakeside Inn. "Other people will look guiltier than me. Blaster, for instance, especially after the business with the tapes. Or maybe, when I finally see Guy again, I'll make it look like he did it."

Nancy shot Colleen a curious glance. "So you don't know where Guy is?" she asked.

"He never said, and I'm in no hurry to see him."

Nancy parked and turned off the ignition. As she and Colleen got out of the car, Nancy cast a longing look at the dark woods bordering the inn. She was too far away to risk running toward the forest, though. Colleen would probably shoot her down before she got there.

"Up the driveway," Colleen directed Nancy, shoving a key in her hand. "Open the front door, then head for the basement."

The front entrance was still sealed with bright yellow tape. Nancy had to peel it off before she could unlock the door. Once the door was open, a burned smell assaulted her nose. The odor grew even stronger as she opened the door to the basement and felt her way down the stairs, with Colleen right behind her.

As Nancy's eyes grew accustomed to the darkness, she was able to make out the distant stone walls and the heaps of charred furniture. Slivers of moonlight crept in through the dusty transom windows.

Nancy looked around for some kind of weapon she could use or an escape route.

"You must have read my mind," Colleen said as Nancy's gaze fell upon several shovels beneath the stairs. "Pick up one of those shovels." When Nancy had obeyed, Colleen directed her to start digging a hole.

Nancy hesitated before plunging the metal blade of the shovel into the hard-packed earth. "What for?" she asked, but the terrible answer came to her before Colleen even opened her mouth.

Nancy was digging her own grave.

"It's the perfect plan," Colleen said proudly. "After you're done digging the hole, you lie down in it and I shoot you. All I'll have to do is throw the dirt back over you, along with Guy's letters and the articles. Then, tomorrow, when the concrete is poured, the evidence will be buried forever."

Nancy shivered. The last thing she intended to do was lie down in the grave and wait for Colleen to shoot her. She'd rather die while trying to run up the stairs. She could only hope that Colleen would make some small slip so she could make a break for it. For now, though, the gun was trained steadily on Nancy, so she dug.

Clink!

Both Nancy and Colleen started at the sound as Nancy's shovel struck something metallic. Scraping away some of the dirt with the edge of her shovel, Nancy saw the corner of a metal box.

"What is it?" Colleen demanded.

"Something's buried here."

"Dig it up," Colleen ordered, an excited look on her face. "Hurry!"

In a few minutes Nancy had unearthed the small metal box, which she handed to Colleen. After opening the box, Colleen removed a few slips of newsprint. "You found it!" she cried triumphantly.

"What is it?" Nancy inquired.

"The articles. Guy buried them! No wonder I couldn't find them. This is my lucky night. I'll be able to get rid of the articles *and* you."

Colleen's expression became deadly serious as she pointed her gun once again at Nancy. "Now, keep digging."

After a while, Nancy had dug a shallow hole about six feet long and three feet wide.

"You know what to do now," Colleen prodded, gesturing with the gun. "Jump in."

Nancy took a deep breath. This was it—her only chance. She moved behind the hole so that it was between Colleen and herself, then started to bend over, as if she were about to put the shovel down. Then, in a sudden, springing motion, Nancy leapt forward, over the hole, toward Colleen, thrusting the blade of the shovel forward like a bayonet.

At the same moment Nancy heard Colleen's gun go off with a deafening explosion.

Chapter

Sixteen

Nancy froze, stunned, as the bullet ricocheted off her shovel and whizzed past her head. Then the air was filled with the sound of shattering glass.

As fragments of glass rained down on the floor, Colleen turned for a split second toward the broken transom window above Nancy. That was all the time Nancy needed.

With a powerful thrust she dived for Colleen's arm, knocking the gun out of her hand. As they fell to the floor, Nancy heard Colleen hit with a thud, then her body went limp.

With a feeling of dread Nancy quickly checked Colleen's pulse, then let out a relieved breath.

Colleen was unconscious, but her pulse was strong. She must have hit her head in the fall.

A moment later Nancy heard loud footsteps rumbling across the lobby floor above. "Nancy!" several voices cried out from the top of the stairs. The work lights in the basement blinked on, and Nancy saw Ned, Bess, and Andrew come running down the stairs. She did a double take when she saw who was with them—Julie Ross!—but she'd have to find out about that later. Right now they had to take care of Colleen.

"How did you find me?" Nancy asked as Andrew picked up the discarded gun and stood over Colleen's unconscious form. He took off his jacket and padded it gently beneath Colleen's head.

Nancy slumped against Ned as he placed his good arm around her and pulled her close. "I got worried when you didn't come back downstairs for a long time," he said, answering Nancy's question. "Then I noticed that Colleen wasn't around, either, so I went upstairs and looked for you. That was when I found your pendant in that little room."

"So Ned came downstairs and got me," Bess continued the story. "When we went outside and saw that one of the garage doors was open, we figured Colleen had taken you somewhere, so we called the police. They sent out a couple of squad cars to look for you."

"It's a good thing we guessed she'd come here," Andrew put in. "One of the police cars should be here any minute."

Nancy showed everyone Guy's blackmail letters and the old articles about the theft ring. "Wow," Andrew said, shaking his head. "I never would have guessed."

"I didn't have time to tell you what we learned at Bentley High School," Nancy told Andrew, "what with the fire and the police taking you in for questioning."

"Ned filled me in on the way here," Andrew told her. He glanced down to where Colleen still lay unconscious, her sequined dress wrinkled and dirty. "I still can't believe it."

"Looking back," Nancy went on, "I realize there were things I didn't pick up on—like all the time Colleen spent in the basement and the fact that she got rid of Lewis's stuff so fast. And all those times she tried to talk you into putting off the renovation for a couple of days."

"Yeah," Andrew agreed. "I guess it wasn't for the kids' safety, like she said. It was so she could have more time to find the articles that Guy Lewis left."

Grinning at Nancy, Bess said, "Leave it to Nan to get to the bottom of things," she said proudly. "She always solves the mystery in the end."

"Speaking of mysteries . . ." Nancy said, turning to Andrew. Julie had gone over to him, and the two were holding hands. "Are you two back together?"

Julie smiled up at Andrew, who leaned down and kissed her tenderly on the lips.

"I guess that answers my question," Nancy said.

"After I got out of the police station this afternoon, I realized how much trouble this inn thing has been and how little I cared about it in the first place," Andrew explained. "So when the police released me, I went straight to Julie's and told her I'd made up my mind. I'm going to stand up to my father, once and for all, and tell him I'm moving to California with Julie."

Nancy was glad to see him looking so determined and happy. "We're going to get married," Andrew went on, "and I'm going to try to make it as an actor. Of course, I didn't know if Julie would say yes or not, after everything we've been through."

Julie hugged Andrew tight. "Of course I said yes. I never stopped loving you, even after I broke up with you."

"Is that why you were hanging around the inn?" Nancy asked. The last pieces of the puzzle were falling into place.

Julie nodded, and her face reddened. "I know there's supposed to be a ghost haunting the place. Well, I guess I was the one haunting it, just to keep an eye on Andrew. I was so afraid he'd meet someone else."

"I knew you two would make up," Ned said.

As Julie looked at Ned, a troubled look came into her eyes. "You might not be so happy when you know what I did, Ned," she said nervously.

"What?" Ned asked.

Julie's gray eyes filled with tears. "I'm the reason you fell off the balcony," she said softly.

"*You* pushed him?" Andrew asked, taking a step back to look at Julie.

"No, of course not," Julie said quickly. "But I was hiding up in the balcony that day, spying on you, and you started walking right toward me. I was so afraid you'd see me, I turned out all the lights!"

"So I *did* slip," Ned said, shaking his head. "I didn't think I'd felt anybody push me."

"Can you ever forgive me?" Julie begged. "If I'd known you were going to fall, I would have left the lights on, even if Andrew had found me. I never meant for you to get hurt."

Ned smiled at Julie. "I can't say I'm happy I fell, but I won't hold a grudge. I know you didn't do it on purpose."

For the second time that day Nancy heard the sound of sirens approaching the inn.

"The police are on their way," Bess said with a relieved smile.

"Uhhhh . . ." Colleen groaned. As everyone turned to look at her, Colleen's eyelids fluttered open.

"Perfect timing," Andrew said, as Colleen groggily tried to prop herself up on one elbow.

Colleen's eyes focused on the group of people towering over her, and she let her head drop back to the ground. "Tell me this isn't happening. . . ."

"It's happening," Nancy assured her. "You made it happen."

The tread of heavy footsteps on the stairs announced the arrival of the police. Nancy saw that Lieutenant Oscarson was the first to reach the bottom. Three other officers were behind her. As Andrew handed Oscarson the gun, Nancy stepped over to the police officer and gave her the newspaper articles, briefly explaining the situation.

"I just wish we knew what happened to Guy Lewis," Nancy finished. "Why hasn't he come forward to get the blackmail money?"

As the other officers helped Colleen to her feet, Lieutenant Oscarson asked Nancy, "Are you Nancy Drew?" When Nancy nodded, the officer said, "I got a call from a Chief McGinnis in River Heights. He seems to be a fan of yours."

Bess and Ned both grinned at Nancy.

"He was asking about this same person," Lieutenant Oscarson went on. Then she announced solemnly, "We've just gotten word that Guy Lewis is dead. He was attempting to burglarize a house the other night, and he fell from a second-floor window. Broke his neck."

151

Colleen let out a gasp. "But . . . why didn't I hear about that?" she demanded. "Why wasn't it in the papers?"

"He didn't have any identification on him," the officer explained. "We had to match his fingerprints to the ones on file, and that took a while."

"So what you're saying . . ." Nancy began as the realization dawned on her.

Oscarson nodded. "Mrs. Morgan went to a lot of trouble for nothing. Her secret would have been safe if she'd just waited it out."

Colleen's whole body shook. "My life is over!" she sobbed as the three officers with Lieutenant Oscarson led her up the stairs. After making arrangements for Nancy and her friends to go to the station to make statements the following morning, Lieutenant Oscarson left.

"Well," Nancy said, turning to her friends, "I don't know about the rest of you, but I'm exhausted."

"Let's go," Ned agreed, taking Nancy's hand.

The group left the inn and headed for the parking lot. But before they could get in their cars, they heard the sound of blaring rock music.

"What's that?" Bess asked as the bright headlights of a car appeared from around the bend. A string of headlights followed the first car, and soon the parking lot was nearly full.

"Blaster!" Nancy shouted as the deejay

hopped out of the first car. "What are you doing here?"

Blaster grinned. "When people started leaving, we figured the party was moving, so we packed up our stuff and came, too!"

His eyes widened as he suddenly noticed Julie standing nearby, hand in hand with Andrew. "I guess you guys got back together," he said gruffly. "I hope you'll be happy."

Then he turned quickly and said to the teens who were getting out of the other cars, "As long as the party's here, there's no reason why we can't keep it going. Let's dance!"

Despite the cold, the teens spread out over the parking lot, moving to the catchy beat.

"Do you want to stay for the party?" Ned asked, looking down at Nancy. "If you're tired, maybe we should leave."

Smiling up at her boyfriend, Nancy said, "You know, I think I'm getting my second wind." Her blue eyes sparkled as she added, "This music's a little fast, though. I was hoping for something more romantic."

"That can be arranged," Ned said. He wrapped his arms carefully around Nancy, and she let her head rest against his shoulder. Then, softly, the two of them swayed together in the parking lot to music that only they could hear.

Nancy's next case:

The director of the National Aquarium in Baltimore asks Nancy to look into a series of threats against his staff. He especially wants her to talk to the curator, Annie Goldwyn, whose stand against industrial pollution has sparked a heated conflict. But before Nancy can meet Annie, the controversial curator meets a violent death!

Was Annie about to expose an illegal polluter . . . or did someone inside the aquarium use the dispute as a cover-up to carry out a personal vendetta? From the exotic aquatic exhibits in Baltimore to the shores of Chesapeake Bay, Nancy looks to close out the case before the sharks close in for another kill . . . in *CROSS-CURRENTS*, Case #68 in The Nancy Drew Files™.